SIMPLICITY

SIMPLICITY

THE JACK HENDERSON STORY

KENNETH KIRSCHNICK

SIMPLICITY
THE JACK HENDERSON STORY

iUniverse books may be ordered through booksellers or by contacting:

iUniverse
1663 Liberty Drive
Bloomington, IN 47403
www.iuniverse.com
844-349-9409

ISBN: 978-1-6632-6731-3 (sc)
ISBN: 978-1-6632-6732-0 (e)

Library of Congress Control Number: 2024920768

Print information available on the last page.

iUniverse rev. date: 09/25/2024

For Dawn, Derrick, Jalen, Madelyn and Hannah...
Life would be very boring without all of you.

Introduction

Have you ever dreamed about the simpler things in life? You will have a hard time believing the things I am about to tell you. You might even think about turning me into the authorities. All I have to say is sit and listen to the story because until you hear everything you might never be able to understand this situation until it happens to you. My name is Jack Henderson. I am now 39 years old, and my life still has its ups and downs.

I met Kenneth Kirschnick about five years ago, when I was sitting at the bar in a great little restaurant called Dapper's. The name of the restaurant has changed, but the food has not. It is located at Cumberland and Belmont in River Grove, Illinois. I was drowning my sorrows in alcohol, and this has become the norm for my current life. It was a deal I made with myself a few years earlier, but I will explain this later.

I was sitting there enjoying my beer, when I happened to look over my shoulder; really a nervous habit; to see Kenneth eating dinner. I know it was a Friday night because Kenneth told me later that he only eats there on Friday nights after work. I recognized him from his first novel, "Jails, Institutions, and Death." I enjoyed the story, but especially liked the photo on the jacket of the book. His photo had made him look very arrogant. Arrogance is something I no longer possess. At times I wish I still could have pride, but my past life experience makes that an impossible trait.

I had been searching for someone who would sit and listen to my story. I figured a writer of fiction would probably be my best possible candidate considering the subject matter. I hoped he wouldn't mind if I asked him for an autograph, and it would be a good icebreaker. I approached his table and asked him if he was Kenneth. He told me he was, and then he invited me to sit with him. At first, we talked about his book, but then I got brave.

I asked him if he would mind if I pitched him a story. He told me he didn't have that much time, but I told him I would tell him the short version. He agreed as long as I kept it less than thirty minutes. Now, the reason this book is titled, "Simplicity: The Jack Henderson Story" and not some catchy biographical title, is because of the content. It might as well be called "The Ramblings of Some Crazy Guy", but there are probably some good reasons why this is not the case. After I explained to Kenneth the basis for the story, he told me he loved it. Then I blew him away with one little tidbit of information I had left out the entire time. I told him it was a true story. Any sane man would have gotten up and paid his bill and left immediately. He didn't react that way, but instead he stared at me for at least sixty seconds. When I just about figured he thought I was crazy, he said, "I'm in." Hence the reason this introduction is not only for you, but for him also.

I want to say thanks to Kenneth for transcribing my events. The deal I made with him was that it would be told in my own words. I am not even getting a cut of the sales. My payment is to have my story told to people without me having to tell everybody, one person at a time. Money means very little to me, which I will explain in a minute. So please do not confuse my story with one of Kenneth's fictional pieces. This book has been written about me, in my own words. Kenneth is not responsible for anything that is said in here. I only ask the reader to please keep an open mind while reading through this book. Let me give you the rundown, and then we can get started.

First off, presently I awake everyday with one priority doing my routine as easy as possible without hurting myself or my "image."

Now you probably think about egos when I say "image," but I am talking about my physical reflection in a mirror. About ten years ago I had everything a man could possibly need or want. I was financially, physically, mentally, spiritually, and emotionally wealthy.

I was married to a beautiful woman named Anna. I had lots of money in the bank. I never got angry because my life was truly perfect in all senses of the word. I started an Internet company in the early '90's. We had invested in an invention that was handed down to me. You may be wondering why an invention would be handed down. Let me explain the back story and then move on.

I knew some people who bred pit bull terriers. They had a really obnoxious puppy. He was so troublesome that they chained him to a radiator every day of his life. The only time he was freed from his bondage was when he could go outside. I was visiting them regularly at the time.

His name was Lil' Jake. I befriended the dog over time, even though he was still obnoxious, we eventually had a routine of our own. I didn't like him being chained up all the time. So, I offered to take him from the owners to give him his freedom. I had a feeling that all he needed was to run in an open field, experience freedom at the basic level, and in the end, he might calm down. I explained all this to the owners. They told me the responsibility of having a pit-bull was great. They tried to explain how rough Lil' Jake could get, but I was not worried. I had a feeling about the dog.

The owners finally agreed to my argument because they had wanted to get rid of him for a long time. It wasn't exactly what I was saying to them that changed their mind, but they knew I would take care of the dog and not hold them responsible for anything that happened after I took over custody. In return, they gave me some old paperwork from an invention that was handed down to them from a distant relative who died. The deal was I would give them a share of the money if I could turn it into something. To make that long story short, I did and kept my promise to them.

As for the dog, Lil' Jake got old, but he was never chained to anything ever again. I let that dog roam free, and I believe he died that way. Freedom is not only a human belief. The animal had a destiny. I gave him the wide-open fields to run through as I had promised the original owners. I fed him steaks and even made him into a stud. He had all his papers stating his heritage. The idea of freedom can touch anything living, which leads me into my story.

I would disclose the invention, but that could allow someone to find the original owners of the idea. I do not want anyone contacted from my old life. You will understand everything more clearly after finishing this book. When I say *we*, I am referring to my partner and I. Also, I will not disclose my partner's name either, this is due to the complexity of this story. Now that the formalities have been covered, I can return to the story.

We were able to secure a substantial amount of investment capital from a few friends who were already successful with the Internet. Our invention was the reason we started the company, but we grew into so many areas of commerce that we couldn't count the money fast enough. Around 1993, I wanted to get married and start a family. I had just turned twenty-five years old, and my college sweetheart was getting antsy. At that time, I talked to my business partner and told him I wanted out. He agreed, and he loved the idea of owning one hundred percent of our business. We agreed on an amount, and I sold my shares of the business. It probably was the best decision I had ever made.

I invested the money in the stock market. I was buying everything from Mutual Funds to Commodities. I put my money wherever my principle would accumulate a good return. I averaged a four percent annual return on my investment over the next decade. This isn't much, but when you figure out the ups and downs of the market it is not that bad. The interest on my principle that I accumulated yearly was around $70,000.00. So now you can do the math and figure out what my partner paid for my share of the company, which if your calculations are correct should be about 1.75 million dollars.

I am sure you are thinking, "Wow, he is a millionaire." Yes, that would be true, but I knew how to use that money to never have to work again. Now, seventy thousand dollars is not that much of a yearly income, but my wife and I lived very comfortably for the first five years of our marriage. Money was not an issue, and we had time to do whatever we wanted.

During this time in my life, I would never use an alarm clock. I went to bed when I was tired, and I slept until I woke up. As for my wife, she is beautiful. We had met in college at San Diego State. Although we are not married any longer, I still love her more than words can describe. I am giving you the details of this story ahead of time, because you will not believe anything from this point onward. When you finish this story, please feel free to send any questions to Kenneth by mail or e-mail. He said he will forward them to me. I will try to respond to every question or letter I receive, but please don't be offended if I do not respond immediately. It only means that I have received a lot of mail, and I will try to answer them as soon as possible. I would tell people how to reach me, but sooner or later someone would try and put me in the psych ward.

Obviously, I know how this story goes. All I ask of you is to please try to understand that this is exactly how it happened in my mind. This letter was written at a request from Kenneth to clarify the story. He didn't want to embellish the facts or make them more believable. I understand his point of view because after he gave me the finished book, I realized that my story is a little hard to follow. I tend to drift from thought to thought. Kenneth did an excellent job with the tenses of my sentences. The past tenses are the story; but the present tenses happen when I lose my train of thought and start to ramble.

Again, I have to thank Kenneth for everything, because he was able to write out my story without changing it. I apologize for the way I tell it, but if you were standing here and I told you the story this is exactly how it would sound. I don't know what your imagination can do for you in deciding whether or not it is true. Ah hell, I guess I should just leave that part for you to decide. In the meantime, you can also wonder if I am crazy or sane. God knows I could use a second opinion.

One last thing, I have become quite the hermit. I am no longer spiritually, mentally, physically, financially, or emotionally wealthy. Instead, I still have some money, but my interest payments are nowhere near where they were five years ago. My wife is gone, and I spend every other week in jail or at the bar. Like I said, it was a deal I made with myself to cause more trouble. You will understand this concept later in the story. The reason I was drinking that Friday night at Dapper's can only be summed up by saying I was looking for trouble. Thanks for being interested enough in my life to buy this book. I hope I can spread the word about these types of extraordinary events.

Sincerely,
Jack Henderson

CHAPTER 1

First, let me start this story in the right direction. I need for you to participate in an experiment. Please walk into your bathroom, or any place with a mirror. Look at yourself. Now lean towards the mirror and look into your reflection's side of the mirror. Now you might be thinking to yourself, "Why am I doing this?" The reason is that when I was a kid, I used to look at my reflection's world and wonder if he was living the same life. Was his side of the mirror the same as my side? Does your reflection's side of the mirror look any different? The answer should be "NO," but in my situation the answer is, "YES!"

I opened my eyes on a very cold Friday morning in December of 1999. The new millennium was two weeks away. I love the cold weather, because of ice-skating, snowboarding, sledding, snowball fights, and building snowmen. Not to mention, Christmas was only a week away and I was looking forward to it. Christmas time at my house was always fun. My wife and I would get together with all our family. We would Christmas shop for our nieces and nephews. We tried to bring the holiday cheer to everyone we interacted with during that time of the year.

My wife was still asleep on that December 17th morning. I looked at the clock and it said, 8:38 AM. It was a good time to wake up. I had nothing to do, and all the Christmas shopping was taken care of weeks earlier. As I mentioned, it was a great time of the year to mingle with the world. For example, I loved the bustling shopping malls and stores with the cheesy music playing over loud speakers.

I put my feet on the floor and slid them into my slippers. They were the fuzzy kind with the fake fur that wraps the top of the foot right below the ankle. My wife always called them girlie, but I loved those slippers. I think I got them as a present a year earlier. It was nice to put warm fluffy things on my feet. It reminded me of my childhood. Christmas time was for children, and it brought me back into that state of mind. This reminds me of another reason to explain my love for the holidays. I remember my mother wearing colorful sweaters on Christmas Eve and Christmas morning. I would never see those sweaters except during this time of the year.

One Christmas morning; way back in the early '80's; I awoke to a freshly covered ground of snow. At least five inches had fallen throughout the night. It was pleasant since I remember the light snowflakes falling down outside my bedroom window. The flakes enveloped the light from the alley streetlights and broadcast it like a film projector showing the latest Hollywood hit right there on my walls and ceiling as I drifted off dreaming about all those wonderful toys I had asked, begged, and pleaded for since Halloween. That morning peering out my second story apartment bedroom window over the snow-covered landscape put me in a trance. This snow-induced coma became more and more intense with every breath. The smell of fresh bacon, and fried eggs crept into my nostrils forcing my brain back into the present. I turned my head just in time to hear my name echoing through the apartment from the kitchen.

I turned and bolted for my bedroom door. I grabbed the door frame with my right hand and slid on the less-girlie slippers I owned as a kid, using the frame as leverage I spun one hundred and eighty degrees into the hallway that spanned my parent's apartment. I tried running for the kitchen, but couldn't get any traction after the smooth slide from my bedroom. The ending result propelled my body into a forward top-heavy fall that caused me to slide head first into the kitchen on my stomach. I did a penguin spin at the end and rolled onto my back looking up at the ceiling from the kitchen floor. There above me was the shadows of my mother's beautiful face, even though it had a look of annoyance, that was ignored by my father's grandiose smile and chuckle that shook his belly like Santa Claus. She shook her head at my father and me, and turned back to the stove to finish placing healthy portions of meat and poultry onto plates for her two men on that glorious Christmas morning. I laughed with my father for a second, but it was short lived as the grandeur of presents in the other room stealthily crept back into my brain.

I rolled over to get up and at the same time I stared down the hallway into the living room to see all my presents lying under our Christmas tree. I pretended like it was taking me a long time to get off the floor. My stare was long and hard as I tried to imagine what those sparkling packages held underneath. I knew the rules, and if I was to get to those gifts from Santa, I would have to be patient, yet vigil. I knew I had to inhale my breakfast as fast as possible, luckily my father was the master at inhaling meals, so I had him on my side as we fought back the patience my mother was well known for. She would be the only blockade that morning, taking her time with her breakfast, forcing my father and I to bite our lower lips while stealing glances from the living room. Those are the memories of Christmas that I cherish the most. Putting on my fuzzy slippers in my adult years still makes me want to run without traction, falling to the ground with hopes of stealing glances towards that place where Santa is most known for, under the Christmas tree.

I slid my feet into my slippers. I stood up and looked out the window. It was gleaming white outside. The frost on the outside of the window looked so pleasant. I stretched my arms like people do in the movies. I know it sounds like a cliché, but that is what I did. I grabbed my robe from the foot of the bed and wandered into the kitchen. I tried desperately to not wake my wife. She was never a morning person. This is just one of the many reasons why I am in love with this woman to this day.

I grabbed the bag of beans off of the counter, and began my morning ritual. I used to prepare the coffee pot before I went to bed, but since I retired, there was not a good enough reason to have coffee; ready-made. I mean I woke up at different times every morning. It would have been impossible to figure out the exact time. So, I just began a new ritual.

I would grab the bag of beans, always beans, never store-bought grounds. I put them in the grinder and then replace the cap. Next, to avoid my wife's wrath, I would go into the garage and grind them up. I can safely assume you might be laughing at me right now in your mind. Let me ask you if you have ever had your significant other get up on the wrong side of the bed? I have and by days end we were not a couple; and that could ruin any person's day. I have had it happen to me quite a few times.

There was this one time when my wife still drank coffee before switching to tea, and I had made just enough noise to awake her, but only made enough coffee for myself. By the time she rolled out of bed, and stomped into the kitchen to have a fresh cup of coffee, there was just a little at the bottom of the pot still burning from the hot burner. Of course, I was content having slurped down four solid cups of strong joe. I felt the heat from her breath breathing onto the top of my head as I lounged in my lay-z-boy. I tilted my head back to see her holding an empty coffee cup. The sight still gives me the chills when I recall it, there was murder in those loving eyes. The worst part was I knew I was going to be the victim.

I wish I could still say I had opportunities to fight with her some more, at least then she would still be a part of my life. However, that is not the case, and I am not going to bore you with a ton of details about loving and losing. Marriage is a work in progress. I just never realized that until it was too late. That woman had every emotion

4

known to mankind, but I loved them all. I just wish I was telling you this and laughing instead of being reminded about the saying better to love and lose than to never love at all, which I think must come from a person that never found love at all.

Coffee grinders are loud when they are grinding the beans. I am sure you have heard the "whirrrrrrrrrrrrrrrrrrrrrrrr" that was my impression for you. The wife hated the sound of the grinder in the morning. She always wanted to buy pre-ground coffee, but I would not drink it. When she tried to get me drinking the name brand stuff, I found myself hitting the local coffee shop. This is not a cheap alternative, but that is nothing you didn't know already though, right?

There I was grinding my beans in my cold garage. The whirring of the blades was lost in the crisp wind blowing against the outer walls. I was able to hear the frozen ice intermingled with the blowing snow make sounds like scattered salt on a smooth, hard surface. The memories of broken glass scattering on pavement after a car accident come to mind when describing the sounds from the outer walls of my garage.

I am getting off the subject, but after a few minutes of grinding beans, it is good to check the quality of the powder. I tapped the top of the grinder and pressed the button once more, just to make sure it was a fine powder. I like my grounds to be almost dust. I don't know, I guess you can say I am a creature of habit. When it comes to coffee grounds, the very fine powder doesn't block the water from flowing into the pot when brewing. The key is to grind those beans, stop, then tap the grounds by pounding the grinder against the palm of your hand. This frees up those grounds stuck underneath the blades. It is very important if you enjoy coffee in its purest form. It may sound tedious and almost autistic in nature, but it is sure worth the effort. After deciding the powder was fine enough, I unplugged the grinder and walked back into the kitchen. Plus, the wind was blowing so hard, I felt the chill all the way in my bones. No fuzzy slippers or thick robe would have kept the chill out that morning. I was happy to feel the warmth of my kitchen on my face, and I approached the stairway to Heaven; I like to call my coffee pot; and poured the grounds out of the grinder.

I loved my pot. It was the kind that used cone shaped filters. I guess I just like things that were less ordinary. Nowadays, everyone has a coffee maker with the cone shaped filter. Just one more thing to add to the list of things I bought before it became the norm. I pressed power and heard the gurgling of the water in the machine. Eight minutes and twenty-four seconds later, I knew I was going to be enjoying my morning cup of Joe. Yeah, I timed it one day. I told you retirement isn't all it is cracked up to be. You do get bored, even with lots of money and time. Those guys that take their money and get barbie doll wives, or live lavish lifestyles, and find themselves on next month's National Enquirer or Star front pages always puzzled me. Boredom is not great, but it sure beats working. Let me know if I am wrong, and I will only listen to those near my age group. Of course, boredom and retirement might not get old if you are post-60's, but here I was in my thirties and it wasn't that bad. I just had to find things to occupy my time.

As for the rest of the house, I would give you a detailed layout of the house, but it is not important right now. A minor description should suffice for the story's sake. My wife and I lived in a Bungalow style, one bedroom house. Sure, we had money, and could afford something bigger, but we had no kids and it was just the two of us. We lived in a regular residential neighborhood called Old Irving Park right in the heart of the city. I call it the "heart" because it made me feel alive. If you asked another Chicagoan though, they might tell you the "heart" was their own neighborhood. I liked it and I am pretty sure she liked it too.

The coffee was brewing, and I needed to brush my teeth. Sometimes I would do that first, but that day I needed a cup of coffee, pronto! I walked into the bathroom and grabbed my brush. Have you ever noticed that it is impossible to put the toothpaste on your brush like they do in the commercials? I mean the way they curl it under itself and over itself. Trust me it is impossible. I spent many days trying to do it. Not to mention; wasted several tubes of paste. Again, "retirement" is all I have to say. I brushed my teeth and after I rinsed, I began to look at my face. I don't know what it is about mirrors, but my face never looks the same.

I know I could have used a razor that morning; the growth on my face was becoming irritating. A man's face itches after a few days without a razor. My wife always loved my face when it was clean-shaven. I really like the rough look. Plus, it is one less thing to do in my busy day. I was standing in front of the mirror, surveying the few scars, beard, and various inconsistencies from my left side of my face compared to the right side. I was startled a knock at the door. I looked over my shoulder expecting to see my wife. The doorway was empty. I stared into the hallway for a few seconds and thought I heard a faint knocking, but it was so distance I thought it was the wind blowing against the house again. I turned back to stare myself down and hopefully lose the urge to shave.

The itching was a bother, but it could be equated to a mosquito landing on your skin and walking around looking for a good place to bite. It usually is annoying, but can be easily dealt with by swatting it away, which is exactly what I did to my reflection. I swatted at the mirror and laughed at myself, because today was going to be a caveman day. No razors, no priorities, I was just going to grab my cup of coffee, sit in my chair and relax. Knowing the holidays were upon me made the whole scenario must easier to handle.

As I left the bathroom, I thought I heard that knock again. At first it sounded like the front door, but then it seemed to also be coming from the bathroom wall behind the mirror. That was an absurd notion, there was nothing behind the mirror, but bricks, insulation, and mortar. I stood there for a minute listening as quietly as possible. The knocks kept coming in spurts, so I wandered out of the bathroom to see if maybe someone was at the front door.

I tried to figure out who would be visiting me at 9 AM. I approached the door without an answer to my initial question of why someone would be visiting me this early. Maybe it was a Jehovah Witness or the Avon lady or even Girl Scouts, all of those visits are fun to me. I like to interrogate the Jehovah's Witnesses, try to sell the Avon lady other products, and I absolutely love Girl Scout cookies. I opened the door and nobody was there. I figured I was just hearing things. I mean without my morning coffee, anything is possible. After closing the door and not giving it a second thought I wandered back into the kitchen and grabbed my favorite coffee mug. My wife bought it for me a few years earlier because it had a nice saying on it. "I haven't had my coffee yet; don't make me kill you!" It is pretty funny how true those greeting card sayings can be, even if it should have been her mug. I loved the mornings, and it was my favorite time to sit and reflect on life in general.

I opened the refrigerator door and grabbed the creamer. I poured in the creamer, and then added the sugar. Then I filled up the rest of my mug with the freshly brewed coffee. I do this because you do not need to stir your coffee. The physics of pouring the hot liquid on top of the creamer and sugar causes everything to mix perfectly. I could go on and on about the coffee thing, but will try and save some of your sanity and stop here.

I walked into our living room and slid into my favorite chair. It was a leather recliner, the soft leather with the big puffy arms. I grabbed the remote control and turned-on Bloomberg Television. That was my favorite part of my day. I knew that every day I turned on my television I could see the stock market. This was great because I was always making money. Sure, some funds do better or worse than others, but when you diversify you level out.

This day was starting out to be like my usual days, but after I polished off a few more cups of coffee I realized I had to burn off the caffeine boost. I went back into the bedroom to throw on some jogging pants and my old college sweatshirt. I grabbed a pullover and another hooded sweatshirt. I mean; anyone who lives here knows that Chicago can be mighty unfriendly around Christmas. I should say the weather not the people. At least I have met some unfriendly Chicagoans, I guess it depends on your circle of friends.

I walked out the front door and breathed in a deep breath of crisp, cold air. My lungs burned for a second, but I love that feeling. I was standing in front of my house and I started to stretch my legs a little bit. It is a good idea to stretch, especially when it is cold. I started jogging down my block towards Elston Ave. I was moving at an even pace. I loved the feeling I get when I run. My brain changes and it relaxes me. At first in the cold weather, it is hard to focus on anything except the cold, but as soon as my body temperature rises, my blood gets pumping, and I feel so much better.

I jogged around my neighborhood for about thirty minutes. I never had a set path I took, instead I liked to just wander around the city blocks and keep the routine irregular. Luckily, the snowfall from a week earlier had totally melted away. Running down sidewalks that had not been shoveled was a pain in my ass. Sorry, I don't swear very often, but some things just get my blood boiling. Like President Bush, okay, I am not going to go there.

So, after I finished running, I realized I was near Irving Park Rd. and Pulaski. It really was not that far from my house, and the Golden Nugget Restaurant across from the Y.M.C.A. building was only few blocks west. So, I figured I could run over there, grab a bite to eat and still make it home before my wife woke up.

I entered the restaurant, asked for a non-smoking table, and ordered a stack of flapjacks, with two eggs over easy, and side of bacon. I just love the taste of pork. The waitress was very nice; I think

9

her name was Ellen. I can't be sure, but she was a great lady. She was definitely going to get a nice tip. She always kept my coffee cup filled, even though I really didn't drink much of it. That in itself; is worth the fifteen percent gratuity. I finished my breakfast. I paid for my food and figured I had better use the bathroom before I dived back into the wind tunnel called Chicago.

I walked into the bathroom. It was dimly lit, and the janitor must have had the day off. My arm got snagged on a giant splinter that was hanging off of the door. It went through all three of my sweatshirts and pierced my skin. I shut the door, swore out loud, and pulled up my sleeve to survey the damage. There was a little blood trickling out of the cut. It was in the pit of my elbow, opposite of my elbow joint. You know where your arm bends? It is the same place doctors put I.V. needles. I checked it in the mirror and then proceeded to wash it off in the sink. Luckily, the splinter didn't get stuck in the skin. Instead, it was still embedded in the thick cotton armor of my sweatshirts. I pulled out the little piece of wood and tossed it into the garbage can. These types of things were always happening to me. It was like I was accident-prone or something. I figured out later, that being accident-prone and having fate's foot up your ass are two totally different things. Sometimes you can only describe life in its most basic sense.

I used the bathroom, checked my reflection in the mirror, and was about to leave, when at that moment, there was another knock at the door. I opened the bathroom door to tell whomever it was that I was finished. To my surprise again there was nobody there. I found that kind of strange that this was the second time in one day. I sat there and stuck my finger in my ear and shook my ear canal. Obviously, that is not a great method for fixing your hearing, but it was my reaction. I left the bathroom and began heading home.

I was hoping I could get home before my wife woke up. My thinking was that she would not be mad that I had breakfast without her if she didn't know I had breakfast at all. She always wanted me to be the good husband, but retiring at such an early age, kept me from acting like an adult most of the time. I still loved to play video games and sports. I didn't have a 9-5, which left me free to do whatever I wanted. The selfishness increased over the years as my ways to spend my days changed. I tried to include her into more stuff, but she didn't always want to have fun like I did.

It was like she wanted to play housewife, but I never left. Not to mention, we paid for a maid. So, there was no need for cleaning. Plus, we did not have any kids. That saved us from having to do extra housework or cooking. I love to eat out and I tried to pass along that same love to her, but she insisted on pushing for home cooked meals. I mean I didn't mind as long as she was the one who cooked. The point was whether or not we paid someone to cook, which is considered a home-cooked meal in her eyes.

The only thing I knew how to make was Macaroni and Cheese. I even messed that up more often than not. We were constantly arguing and complaining about the other person's idea of a loving home. I love her, and I know she loves me, but we were not on the same level. Thinking about it now, since I am telling you, I could have been more understanding. I should have been more adjustable in my behavior and thought patterns. Hell, we would probably still be married today if I was that way. I just didn't understand how to be that way until she was gone. If I could go back in time, things would be a lot of different between us. My love for her has grown, and my irresponsibility as an adult is minimal, with the exception of the deal that I have with myself today. Okay, I should probably get back to the story.

So, I walked home, because I was tired of running, and my thighs were sore because I hadn't run for a couple of days. That is just another consequence of early retirement. I never had a set schedule. I got home about a half hour later. It was almost 11 AM. I figured she would be up. I walked in and immediately smelled eggs and bacon. The smell was strong and I knew I had better lie about where I had been because I didn't want to fight or argue. She would not be happy if I told her I already ate. I entered the kitchen and there she was in her dark brown robe, cooking breakfast for the both of us.

My beautiful Anna was cooking and trying to be the good housewife. She was always a sight for sore eyes. She is about five foot nine, long dirty blonde hair, eyes that could pierce my soul, a smile that brightened and warmed me, and a very beautiful backside. That was always my favorite feature to stare at. I haven't seen her in about three years, but she never lost that beauty. God, I miss her…

Sorry, we have to move on because whenever I think about my ex-wife, I tend to lose my train of thought. I sat down at the table and we had a very nice breakfast. I wasn't very hungry obviously, but I ate as much as I could just to save face. She asked me how my run was. I told her it was very cold outside. I changed the subject into some other conversation about our finances and she quickly stopped talking. I always knew how to stop her from asking any more questions. She hated it when I talked about the stock market. It was one of her pet peeves.

We finished up breakfast and then we cleaned up by washing the dishes. She washed and I dried. Afterwards, Anna said she was going to take a shower, so I returned to my stock market. I could spend every waking minute watching my money grow. I actually did spend a lot time in front of my television or on the phone with my broker. I would see something I liked or disliked and I had my broker on speed dial. The conversations would be quick because there was never any reason to have small talk with him. It was all about the money, and that is why I liked him so much.

Anna finished up in the bathroom and I was pretty ripe myself from the run, so I jumped in the shower after she was finished. It was a good idea that I washed out the cut from the restaurant. If my wife would have seen the blood, then she would have started questions and her form of interrogation. I was not ready for that kind of interrogation because it always resulted in an argument. She could be quite the little detective. I was in no mood to be given the silent treatment either. We had planned that night, and I wasn't going to ruin our day with one of my selfish acts. Let me tell you that I am very capable of being selfish quite a lot. The rest of that day was really uneventful, but the night was just heating up.

CHAPTER 2

My wife had bought tickets to go see a comedian at Zanies comedy club. I was not that interested but marriage is a give and take commitment for life. We got all dressed up that evening and made our way to the club. Her plan was to have a nice dinner at Edelweiss. For those of you who are not familiar with Edelweiss; I will fill you in. It is a great German-American cuisine restaurant on Irving Park Rd. It is just west of Harlem Ave. on Irving Park Rd. in Norridge. I recommend it to anyone who might enjoy German cuisine. They have a wide range of German beers on tap and in the bottle. Their schnitzel is top notch. Not to mention all the meats and other delicacies you can think of from that culture.

We had a wonderful time at the restaurant. I love to drink German beer out of the stein. I know you are thinking, Henderson is not a German name, but actually my mother was full-blooded German. Her parents; my grandparents; came to America after WWII. My mother was born here, and my father had a mix of cultures, so I don't even bother trying to figure out his heritage. I love German food and beer. As for the lederhosen, I could care less, but give me Oktoberfest any day of the week.

We had a great meal and headed down to Zanies. The comedian was funny. I just don't mean "ha ha" either. This guy was hilarious. I was laughing so hard at one point; my stomach was cramping up. If there is one thing in this world that I adore, it is humor. I love to laugh, and I always knew that humor is the best healing method known to man. There is another great physical feeling that happens when you know you are laughing too hard and that is when you awake the next morning and your cheeks hurt.

I know everyone has normal days that they can recall. However, this day was far from normal, which is why I started here instead of at the middle of my story. The comedian finished his performance, and I figured I had better use the bathroom before we headed home. It was not that long of a drive, but it was late, and if I had to go on the way home, I would be shit out of luck.

I went to the bathroom, while my wife went to retrieve the car from the parking lot. I told her I would meet her outside in a minute. I hate driving. Why drive when you can be chauffeured? I opened the bathroom door, headed for the urinal and took care of my business. I finished up and went to the sink and washed my hands. Now this is where my life changed permanently. When I say permanently, I do mean every day since has been a nightmare. There is no going back to before that day in my mind. This is why the day I have just explained is so crisp and fresh in my mind.

I looked into the mirror to make sure my hair was in place. Not that I was trying to impress anyone, but it always helped my ego to look good no matter where I was at the time. I heard the knock on the door again. Except this time, I finally realized that it was coming from the other side of the mirror. I looked down at the sink to regain my composure. I thought I was going crazy. I noticed there was blood soaking through my shirt. I unbuttoned my sleeve in such a hurry and that is when I realized that my fresh cut had opened up. I began to wash it out immediately. At that point, I totally forgot about the knock from the other side of the mirror. When the cut from the sliver stopped bleeding, I looked at myself again. I was very confused.

I put my finger up to the mirror just to see if I was on some Candid Camera thing. I mean, I was in a comedy club after all. Who knows what kind of tricks they would pull there? The minute

I touched the mirror, my whole world changed. I can't explain it very well, but I will try. In a split second, I was on the other side of the mirror. I blinked, and when my eyelids went up, I was staring at myself in the flesh. My reflection was no longer a reflection. He was flesh and blood. He was something I could touch, smell, and hear. Obviously, you can always see your reflection in the mirror, but when have you been able to stand side by side yours?

He said, "Don't get weird on me, I need your help."

I was so confused I was speechless. I realized after a few seconds that my mouth was hanging open. How would you react to this? I just got pulled through a mirror. I looked back at the mirror, and I had no reflection. There was nobody on the other side; just an empty bathroom. My reflection and I were standing in the same room, but we could touch each other. Normally, I would have screamed, but I thought I was dreaming or had entered The Twilight Zone. I am still trying to figure that out today! To this day, it still doesn't make sense to me. I will never be able to explain it any better than this. If this explanation is hard to understand, please keep going and hopefully it should become clearer.

"Look, I need you to open that door and stall for time while I flush this stuff down the toilet." He said.

I looked down and he had this package of drugs sitting on the urinal. Now you are probably asking what kind of drugs? Well, so was I! So, he walks into the stall and I hear the toilet flushing. I didn't know what to do. That is when I heard someone knocking again. Now that I am thinking about it, I think they were knocking the whole time he was talking to me, but in my confusion, I must have blocked out the sound.

I unlatched the bolt on the door and immediately I was thrown back into the wall behind the door. A police officer comes rushing past me into the bathroom. I stood there as he flew past me. I went to leave the bathroom and that is when another police officer stopped me. I was thrown up against the wall face first. He held his forearm in the back of my neck. After about two minutes, the other cop comes out of the bathroom.

The first cop says, "I can't find anything."

"He must have flushed it." The cop holding me against the wall said.

I looked down the corridor of the hallway and notice that I was not even in the comedy club anymore. It was some dank coffee shop. There were no patrons, just some fat chef with a stained greasy shirt reading a newspaper while he smoked on a fat cigar.

I don't think you can understand how confused I was.

"Where are the drugs?" The cop yelled into my ear as he applied more pressure on my neck.

"I have no idea what you are talking about?"

"Don't give us that bullshit; you junkie scumbag!" The other cop yelled.

"Seriously, there was some other guy in there. I don't know where he went!"

I was seriously confused by this time. I really didn't know if I had seen myself or someone that looked like me. I did remember the comedy club though, which told me that this was becoming a weird dream.

They put me in handcuffs and escorted me out to their cop car. I was sitting in the passenger seat of the squad car, while they ran my identification in the computer. I figured I was dreaming. Seriously, how else can I explain, getting sucked through a mirror, meeting my reflection, then being practically arrested? Not to mention, my reflection disappeared after I saw him go into the stall.

"So, if you really don't know anything; why do you have a fresh track mark?" The cop spitted as he pointed to my open cut.

"I got that at the Golden Nugget earlier today when I bumped into the bathroom door."

17

"Oh, so you are dealing out of multiple locations huh?"

"No."

"Shut up, I don't want to hear any more of your shit." The cop yelled from the front seat. He laid his gloved hand smack across the back of my head.

"Now fess up. It will be much easier if you do."

"I am not saying anything else until I see a lawyer. I know I have rights."

"How's this for rights?" The cop outside of the car pulled me from the front seat and threw me up against the back of the squad car. He opened the back door and threw me in. The door slammed behind me as my face was securely planted on the fake vinyl of the seat. I think any normal person would have reacted the same way I had considering the circumstances.

I finally realized I had better shut my mouth until I could figure out what was going on. I ended up being arrested for some outstanding traffic warrant. I never ever got a ticket for driving in my entire life. Well, once I got a speeding ticket, but it was dropped in court. I knew the wrong information about me was popping on the cruiser's computer. The only problem would be for how long would the wrong information keep me from my freedom?

They took me to their police station. They put me in a jail cell. Let me tell you about jail cells. I had never been in one before that day, and it is no picnic. There is a concrete slab on one side and a metal toilet on the other. They both didn't look very comfortable. After some experimenting, I found that neither one of them *are* comfortable.

"We are going to file this paperwork. Hopefully you got more on you than just a traffic warrant." The cop snarled as he slammed the cell door.

I ended up falling asleep on the concrete bench. There wasn't even a mirror in the cell. I can tell this story now because I have had a few years to reflect on my memories. Now you might not understand this, and I know I sound crazy, but I am not crazy. Let me continue explaining the whole story and this part will be clear as day to you.

I woke up from my little nap. I looked over and saw my clock on my night stand read 2:14 AM. I turned my head and that is when I felt so relieved. Anna was sound asleep next to me. I quietly got up and walked through my house. Yep, I was home. It was just a dream. The weird thing is the dream was the most real thing I had ever felt while sleeping.

I walked over to the laundry basket and found the shirt I was wearing at the comedy club. I picked it up and saw the blood stain on the sleeve. That is when I reached into the pocket of my shirt and found the two ticket stubs from the club. I felt a little better, because that was obviously real. I still needed to figure out what happened on the trip from the comedy club to my house.

I tried to get it out of my mind, but the words of my reflection telling me "He needed my help" kept repeating itself over and over in my head. I had a hard time falling back to sleep. I got up and made myself a bowl of cereal. Whenever I could not sleep, I loved to get a midnight snack. I could reflect on whatever was bothering me. I just stood there in the kitchen next to the sink for what seemed like hours; I never even turned the kitchen lights on.

Luckily, the streetlights illuminated the dark kitchen just enough to see. The cereal was tasty, and so I decided to pour myself a second bowl. I stood there trying to think of other things besides my reflection, but the idea of me even contemplating helping my reflection kept popping into my head. It had to be a dream; I had thought over and over. I know that things like this do not happen to regular, every day, sane people. It was sending shivers throughout my body. I could feel the goose bumps on my forearms. That is when I tossed my cereal bowl into the sink ran the water over the empty bowl and left the kitchen.

I knew I was tired enough to sleep, at least, until the sun came up. I crawled back into bed. I still didn't fall asleep right away, but I was starting to feel calmer. The last time I looked at the time on the clock; that I can remember was 4:18 AM. It was a long time before my eyelids became heavy, but then the feeling of sleepiness finally over took me. I have to say it could not have been too soon. Then there was darkness and all was well, okay not really.

CHAPTER 3

6:53 AM. I was pissed when I saw those numbers. I had not seen 7 AM. on the clock in years. The problem I always had; and still do to this day; is whenever I open my eyes and the sun is up it forces me to be awake for the rest of the day. I can't sleep with the light on either, I guess it has something to do with being able to see the light through my eyelids. It is just one of those things I cannot control. So, it was the same routine all over again, fuzzy slippers, stretching, robe, and straight to the coffee pot. I would tell you all about it, but you already know.

That second day, I needed a cup of coffee more than I had in any months prior that I could remember since retiring. I could feel a headache beginning right above my eye. I had not had a headache in years. I used to get really bad ones when I was still working. That was another reason I wanted out of my business. The stress of owning your own business is murder unless you like chaos. I was never a big fan of drama. As a matter of fact, I would like to think that I live in a drama-free zone.

I didn't run to the garage that day. I ground up the beans right there in front of the coffee maker. I was not thinking about the wife, or anyone else. I was in one of my selfish moods. This is not a good thing for everyone else around me. It is fine for me, but when I get like that you might want to look out. I have lost many friends because of days like that.

The whirring of the grinder didn't wake my wife. Not that I

would have cared much if it did. I poured the water into the maker and then I opened the filter to pour in the coffee. This is where I totally lost my mind. Stuffed into the filter area of the maker, was a little folded piece of paper.

I put down the ground coffee, and grabbed at the paper like a little kid who finds a quarter on the sidewalk. I looked around the kitchen and outside, I don't know why, but I felt like someone was watching me. Now, this is what the little note said:

I told you I needed your help. Thanks for giving me the time I needed but I still need a really big favor. I will see you in a few minutes. I know you got to brush your teeth now. We can talk then and don't worry I am not going to put you into anymore-crazy situations, like last night.

Now as you can see, I was a little nervous about this note being in my coffee pot. Not to mention; it was my handwriting. I started ripping up the note because I was afraid, and I didn't know what was happening. I tell you the last thing I wanted to do was to be going into the bathroom to brush my teeth, which is why I stuffed the ripped pieces of paper into my robe pocket. After that I poured the grounds into the maker, and hit the power button.

Someone was playing a mean joke on me and this is why I waited for the coffee maker to brew only two cups. I poured myself a cup without letting it finish. I did that very rarely. The reason is when you take the first cup of coffee out of the pot before it is done brewing you get the strongest cup. This makes the rest of pot taste like colored water. There is no flavor in the rest of the pot because you take the strongest part. But the upside to this theory is that is where all the caffeine is hiding. And I needed a serious caffeine boost that day.

I drank it black that day. I needed to get the caffeine in my body, hence no reason for creamer or sugar. I felt horrible and I probably didn't look too good either. I would have checked, but I was afraid of looking at myself. I am sure if you were in my shoes, you wouldn't have wanted to go anywhere near a mirror either. I went into the living room and slid into my chair.

I turned on the television, but since it was Saturday, the markets were closed. I turned on the news and tried to keep my mind from racing with all these different questions. The worst part about questioning yourself is you usually do not have the answers to those questions. Robert DeNiro in the movie "Ronin" says it best, "Whenever there is doubt; there is no doubt." I think that hits the nail on the head. If you truly doubt something, then it was never for sure in the first place. Which is a great motto to live by, but not when you are questioning your own sanity. I mean, does a crazy person know he's crazy, or does he think he is sane, and assumes everyone else is crazy? There are a lot of philosophical questions I would love to have answered.

I drank cup after cup like it was water. The other cups definitely tasted like water, because of my haste. But the coffee began to kick in and I calmed down. I started telling myself that I was just over-reacting to the situation, and the events that happened the night before were just a dream. I made another pot of coffee, and the clock read 8:12 AM. I figured it was time to clean myself up.

I wandered into the bathroom and looked at myself. It was still me! I started making gestures to myself. I was laughing and talking to myself in the mirror. It is pretty comical now that I think about it. Imagine an experience like the night before happening to you. How would you react the next morning? I was thinking my wife must have written the letter in the coffee pot. I mean there had to be a good explanation for all of this, and when she woke up, I would get to the bottom of the entire situation.

I brushed my teeth and jumped into the shower. The water was hot and I felt better. I took one of those long, hot showers. The kind that fogs up the mirror, and there is that haze of steam that just hangs

23

in the bathroom. I couldn't see myself in the mirror when I exited the shower because of the steam. I chuckled out loud many different times. I dried off, and watched the steam dissipate. I stood there naked in front of the mirror. My reflection was just *my* reflection.

I put my head up against the mirror and looked around the corner to see the shower. It was the same shower. I kept laughing at myself throughout the entire routine. I was acting really silly or crazy, depending on whom you are talking too. A split second later I was staring at myself in the flesh again. I looked at the mirror and there was no reflection. I was staring at myself again. I mean…give me a second here, and let me try to figure out how to explain this better.

Okay, I guess the best way to explain this is to just tell you exactly what happened. I mean if I give you the details then maybe you can visualize the situation in your own mind. I reached my hand out and touched myself. I could feel the skin of my reflection in front of me. I snapped my arm back so fast and I fell backwards into the wall.

"Whoa, relax man. I thought you would have been all right with this by now. We may look alike, but we definitely don't think alike. Look, have a seat on the toilet and I will try to make this as fast as possible. I know you got Anna on the other side and if I was you; I would never have gotten out of bed."

My reflection stood there talking to me, like I was a different person. I really can't explain it any better than that. I sat down on the toilet and put my hands over my eyes. I didn't want to believe anything. I didn't know what to believe. I figured I was going crazy and I was going to see a doctor as soon as possible.

"Quit thinking like that, doctors are not going to help you or me."

I looked up and realized he had heard my thoughts, but I didn't say it out loud. I looked into his eyes; the same eyes I have been staring at for thirty years and saw me, yet I still only saw "me"!

I asked, "What the hell was going on?"

I felt like I was out of place for the first time in my entire life.

"Okay! Obviously, I am your reflection. This much is true, and no; you are not crazy. I gave you a taste of my life last night. Let me also say, that I took a taste of your life last night." He grinned and laughed. "Sorry, I didn't mean any offense by that." I didn't know what he meant by that comment at the time but I understand today.

"I screwed up, and I would never have involved you in my dealings, but I have no other options right now. So, I need to take care of some shit on your side today, which means you have to stay here."

I didn't like listening to myself order me around. Wait, that didn't sound right. Okay let me just finish telling you what he, I mean I, ah whatever, moving on!

He paused for a second, and then finished giving me his *orders*. "Just stay in the room, and meet me back in this bathroom at 5 PM. It really is not that difficult to follow my instructions. Don't start thinking that you are dreaming or that this is some kind of prank someone is playing on you, because none of that is true. You need to stay in this room, and meet me back here at 5. Cool?"

I laughed out loud, and was about to tell him he was crazy, and so was I for that matter. But I never got the chance. I looked up, and he was gone. I turned and faced the mirror, and my reflection was back on the other side. I knocked on the mirror, and it was solid.

I laughed at myself, and just figured I drank too much coffee. My mind was playing tricks on me and I was not going to stand for it any longer. I decided to go wake Anna up and tell her I needed to go to the hospital. I opened the bathroom door and walked out.

To my surprise, I was standing in a motel room. There was an unmade bed in the middle of the room. The lighting was really dim. The drapes were pulled across the window. They were the long kind. You know, the kind that drape from the ceiling down to the floor. The material was thick, like burlap. You could tell that they were old, the kind of curtains that you would see in those old '70's movies.

The wallpaper was a perfect match to the curtains. I looked

around the room and the walls had that gold leaf pattern that was stenciled over the striped wallpaper. I felt like I had walked onto the set of some random porn film.

There was a kitchenette off to my left, with a mini refrigerator in the corner next to the countertop. I noticed the door next to the bay window was locked up tight. The chain, deadbolt, and handle were all locked. I wandered over to it with a renewed energy.

I was confused, I will tell you that, but I was going to get to the bottom of this immediately. I opened the door and the sun blinded me. The parking lot of the motel was practically empty except for a work van parked in the corner of the lot. There were about ten parking spaces. There was one in front of every motel room. There also was a second floor to the motel. The landing shielded the sun a little bit. The burst of cold air froze me instantly. I could feel the droplets of water on my body beginning to freeze as I stood there in the doorway.

I jumped back when I saw a cleaning cart pass by my door. The Spanish cleaning lady came into view. She looked at me and then looked down at my mid-section. She started grinning. I looked down and realized that I was still naked. Even though it was chilly out, I hadn't realized I never put my boxers back on. I just hope her smile was a good thing and not a bad smirk. Yes, the cold air doesn't help the ego of a man when he is standing in front of a woman. Things do shrink, even though I have been told that women do not actually believe this little bit of information. I will leave that truth for you to decide!

I quickly shut the door, and looked around the room for something to put on. I checked the dresser and there were no clothes in any of the drawers. I walked over to the closet and found a suitcase. I opened it up and found my clothes. All the clothes in the suitcase were the same clothes I had in my drawers and hanging in my closet. I grabbed a pair of boxers and a t-shirt. I quickly threw them on and sat down on the bed. If I didn't figure out what was happening to me soon, I felt like I might never be able to figure it out.

I sat on that bed for a long time. I was wishing and praying that all of this was just a dream. The longer I sat there, the more I realized that this was real. I got dressed and looked at the clock. My reflection told me, 5 PM. Now, I know how that sounds, but I am serious when I say; I totally agree with your disbelief right now. But I have to continue because it was as real as anything I had ever experienced up to that point in any moment of my entire life.

I kept telling myself 5 PM, so that gave me a little over eight hours to check out some things. I opened the door and entered a new world. Last night, I remembered being here, but I spent it in a cop car and a jail cell. I thought that was all a dream, but every second that passed was making me realize that might not be the truth. I had to see for myself what was going on.

I made sure I had my room key and wallet. The first thing I needed to do was get home. I stood there in the parking lot checking out my surroundings. I looked up at the sign on the corner. It read "Esquire Motel," and I knew exactly where I was standing. It was not very far from my house. I was on the corner of Elston and Milwaukee avenues. I headed east following Elston Avenue towards Central. I thought I could find a cash station along the way and check the balances in my accounts.

The whole neighborhood is residential except for a couple of bars and restaurants. By the time I realized that none of them had a cash station, I had already reached the corner of Elston and Central. Nowadays, there is a cash station in almost every business, but back then banks were the main locations of such machines. Times sure have changed. I stood there on the corner watching the cars drive by, and I was starting to get cold. I never walked from Milwaukee Avenue to Central down Elston Avenue before. It is quite a long walk.

I wanted to stop and get a bite to eat, but I was more interested in getting to my house. I was cold, and so I kept watching for a cab to drive by. Finally, I reached the bus depot on Elston and Bryn Mawr. I walked up Bryn Mawr and figured I would catch the southbound Central bus that would take me into Jefferson Park Terminal. From there, I could catch the "L" train to the Irving Park Rd. station. I waited and felt the cold wind blowing from the north. It felt like forever, but I guess I just wasn't used to walking around when I needed to go somewhere. This was becoming quite the head-trip.

The bus finally pulled out of the depot and headed towards me. The doors opened in front of me and I climbed up the steps.

"How much is a transfer?" I asked.

"1.75." He replied without hesitation.

I reached for my wallet and opened it up. This is when I realized that I had a wallet full of hundreds. There were not any smaller bills than that. I looked at the bus driver holding a hundred in my hand.

"I don't have change." He pointed to the sign on the money machine. *Bus Driver Has No Change!*

I would never have done what I did that day, but I was in the middle of a life changing experience. I put that hundred-dollar bill into the machine, and the bus driver chuckled at me, like I was the stupidest guy he had ever seen. Let me tell you, I agree with him one hundred percent. I still agree with my stupidity to this day.

I got my transfer and sat down in the back where I could collect my thoughts without having to look at the bus driver any longer. The bus traveled up Central to Milwaukee Ave. where it turned towards Jefferson Park. We pulled into the terminal, and I exited in the back because of the hundred-dollar bill incident.

I ran across the bus thoroughfare, which is illegal, but I did it anyway. Actually, I would venture to say that nobody actually reads that sign saying it is illegal. I was in no mood for anything. I sprinted down the long corridor into the "L" station. I put my transfer into the machine. For a split second I remembered a story I was told about paper transfers being the norm in Chicago. They had switched over the system just a few years earlier. I heard a train rolling underneath me. I ran downstairs to the platform. I jumped on the train and found a seat next to this tiny Asian woman. She obviously was traveling because she had her luggage with her.

There were numerous people on the train, some with Christmas shopping bags, and others with luggage. I normally would have taken a minute to observe my surroundings, but nothing looked out of the ordinary. Everything was the same as I remember and this is why I was beginning to second guess my sanity.

The train stopped at Irving Park and I jumped off. I ran home; and no; I did not stretch. I was running so hard that I got a cramp in the back of my thigh, so I guess I should have stretched. I finally made it home. I stood there in front of my house and ran up the steps. I didn't have any keys except the motel key, so I rang the doorbell. Anna would be able to take me to the hospital. I could be sedated and hopefully the doctors would tell me I had a brain tumor or something. As bad as that sounds, at least I would know that everything that was happening to me was not real. I desperately needed to be told that what I was experiencing was a hallucination or it was a sick joke being played on me.

Anna never came to answer the door. I sat on the front steps blowing into my tightened fists. I should have looked for some gloves at the room. But I didn't. Hindsight is 20-20. I looked down my block and saw the mailman coming towards me. Up the steps and down the steps, house to house, and I watched in anticipation of seeing somebody I knew. The mailman arrived.

"Hello, Dewayne." I said.

He looked at me with a strange expression. He asked me if I knew him. I told him it was me, Jack Henderson. He said he didn't know me, and walked past me to put the mail in the box. I jumped up and immediately grabbed the mail out of the box. He asked me what I was doing. I told him I was checking my mail.

He put his hand on his mace can that was on his belt buckle. I looked at the name on the first envelope, and it was Sherri Crantz. I thumbed through the rest of the mail, and it was all the same name.

"This is not my mail."

"I know that, it is Ms. Crantz' mail. Now put it back in the box. I think you should leave before something bad happens." He said while thumbing his mace can on his belt.

"Now why would I leave my own house?"

That made me a little angry. He removed his mace can from his belt. I put the mail in the box and stepped towards him with my hands up in a passive gesture.

"Get the hell out here, I am calling the cops." He raised his voice while pointing the can of mace at me.

I lost it. I started yelling at him. "This is my house. Where is my wife? Have you lost your mind Dewayne?"

"Have you? I don't know how you know my name, but you have five seconds to get out here." He raised the can towards my face as he screamed back.

I did not hesitate at that moment. I pushed him away from me and he lost his footing on the last step. The snow on the front lawn broke his fall and I ran through my gangway into my backyard. I looked over my shoulder and yelled, "Sorry," as loud as my cold breath could muster as I ran away through the yard. He ran off down the block, and I tried to focus on my surroundings.

I didn't want to take any chances, so I ran out to the alley. I wasn't headed in any special direction. I just needed to find someplace to stop and reflect. I didn't want to be found by the police in case he seriously was going to call them on me. I found out later that it is a federal offense to accost a postal worker. So please don't do it.

I started hopping fences and staying off the streets. An old lady throwing out her garbage yelled, "Why are running through my yard? Damn hooligans."

She startled me enough to lose my focus, and I slipped on a patch of ice. I screamed out in pain, jumped up and ran out of the yard. When I finally realized where I had run too, I needed to find some place close and secure for me to catch my breath. Not to mention, a place to nurse my arm. I ended up at the Shell station on Irving Park Rd. and Pulaski Rd.

I walked in and asked, "Can I use the bathroom?"

The cashier replied, "It's for customers only."

I pulled out my wallet and gave him a hundred-dollar bill. "There, that should cover it. Call it a deposit, I don't care."

He gave me the key. I ran out the store and across the parking lot to the little building in the corner of the lot. I opened the door and shut it behind me. I tried to see into the mirror, but I couldn't because the mirror was all scratched up with graffiti. I could only see pieces of my reflection.

I looked at my eyes. Then I put up my hand to the mirror, and realized I was giving myself the thumbs up. I looked at my hand and there it was, the thumb sticking up. I didn't understand any of this. Then I looked into the mirror, and my reflection was pointing to his wrist, which is what I was doing, obviously. I was losing my mind, one second at a time. I understood he was telling me about the time.

5 PM went through my mind, and I looked at the sink as I slammed my palms onto the porcelain. That was a bad idea. At that moment is when I realized I had broken something in my right arm, it must have happened when I slipped on the ice. The excruciating pain tore up my arm from my hand. I pulled my arm back fast and grabbed at the pain with my left hand. Tears began to roll down my cheeks.

Now, I normally don't cry, but the situation was becoming dire. I didn't know what was happening. I didn't know why it was happening, but I was literally going crazy. I have tried to explain this as normally as I could. If I sound crazy to you, maybe I am, but I am going to continue to tell you exactly what happened next as best as I can.

I tried to stop my eyes from tearing up from the pain of my broken arm. I calmed down and realized that I had better get out of this neighborhood before the cops found me. I was positive the mailman was not going to forget about me pushing him down the steps. I ran back inside the gas station dropped off the key and then bolted across the street to the "L" platform.

I headed back to Jefferson Park. I jumped off the train and ran up the stairs and back down the corridor. When I reached the bus thoroughfare, I looked around and saw a bank across the street. Just to put it in perspective, Jefferson Park Bus terminal is a gigantic piece of property. The thoroughfare has about a dozen or so bays for the different bus lines that cross here. Not to mention the bays cross over into two separate sections. There is a Metra stop above the station, the "L" below, and this wide-open space for buses, which is where I was standing. If you are not familiar, then be my guest and see it for yourself. It is the where Milwaukee intersects with Higgins, Lawrence, and The Kennedy Expressway.

The bank was a great place for me to start getting some other questions answered. Luckily, I was still me, regardless of what was happening. The clock on the sign read 12:15 PM. I still had a few hours until 5 PM. I ran across Milwaukee Avenue and entered the bank.

There was a cash station in the foyer. I pulled out my wallet and grabbed my bankcard. The sight of my card made me feel a little better. I put my card in the machine and typed in my password. My accounts came up in front of me. In the time it took for the machine to process the information, I noticed my reflection in the screen. My reflection was there with me, but I could only look at it. I touched the screen to see if I could somehow change things back, but nothing worked. When I touched the screen, I prompted the ATM to make selections I didn't want, an "Insufficient Funds" message came onto the screen. After realizing I couldn't touch my reflection, I went back to checking my accounts.

The machine asked me which accounts I wanted to access. I pushed my savings account and that is when my world came crashing down around me. My account balance was $12.72, which was impossible. I know I had thousands in the bank. I checked my checking account and I got the same information, except the amount was a little lower. I started sweating and getting dizzy. I pushed the finish button and pulled out my receipt. I looked at it and then I felt my face getting really warm. I stuffed the receipt into my pocket and walked outside for some fresh air.

Whenever I felt nauseous, all I needed was something cold. I still felt a little dizzy, and then everything went black. I fell over and felt the pain of the concrete for a split second.

Opening my eyes, the ceiling slowly came into focus. I looked around the room, and I was back in my bedroom. I checked the clock, and saw it was 3:38 PM. I started freaking out immediately. 5 PM kept flashing in my mind. If it wasn't 5 yet, then where was I? It looked like I was back home, but I couldn't be sure.

"Anna! Anna! Anna!" I yelled from the bedroom.

She came running into the bedroom. "What is wrong with you?"

"I don't know. I just don't feel well and I want to go to the hospital."

She felt my forehead and said, "You are burning up."

She ran to get the thermometer from the bathroom. She put it in my mouth and timed it. When she pulled it out and saw the number, her mouth dropped open.

"Get dressed," she said with such urgency, that it caught me off-guard.

She helped me out of the bed and put on my jacket. She held my arm as I stumbled to the garage.

"Where's your sling?" She asked.

This confused me because I don't remember telling her about my accident with the ice. I remained silent after that question, because I really didn't know what else to do. She put me in the car and we drove out of the garage. She went to pull down my sun visor, and I realized there was a mirror in there. I slammed it back up before I could see myself.

"Look at yourself." She said to me.

"NO! I don't want to look at myself." I screamed at her with all the energy I could muster.

She didn't say one more word all the way to the hospital. She ran into the emergency room, and came out less than a minute later with a nurse and a wheelchair. They wheeled me into the E.R. They tried to cool me down.

"Have you been hallucinating?" The nurse asked me.

"Yes, I have."

"When did it start?"

"It started yesterday?"

"Sir, are you sure? You were here earlier and you seem to be fine."

"No, it started yesterday, I am sure of it! Last night at the comedy club."

Anna chimed in, "Honey, you were fine on the way home from the comedy club."

"No, I was not, actually I have not been alright for over..." I gagged on my own saliva from yelling, "for over a day now!" I yelled back hoping to stop all the questions.

I was so relieved to finally get my answers. I had a bad fever; the temperature had reached 104 degrees. It was such a relief, that I didn't even care about the E.R. thing. I just laid back and fell asleep. Answers are great when they come at the right time.

The sleep I had was so relaxing. Maybe it was the drugs they gave me, but I like to think it was finding that peace of mind. I wasn't going crazy. That was worth any amount of money. Peace of mind is priceless.

I was still in the E.R. when I opened my eyes. There was an I.V. in my arm, and my wife was sleeping in the chair next to my bed.

"Anna." I gurgled out, but I realized that I had a tube stuffed down my throat.

It was a ventilator, and I don't know what time it was because it was so bright in the E.R., and there are never any windows in emergency rooms. I don't know if you have ever been in a hospital emergency room before, but it is hard to tell time. The curtains, separating my room from the nurses' station were closed, and I could not see any clocks. I reached out to touch Anna, and she awoke immediately.

She jumped up and hugged me. I looked into her eyes and saw tears forming. She kissed me on the cheek so lovingly, that I remembered why I retired early. That woman is the epitome of love. I tried to speak again but couldn't.

Anna told me, "Shhh."

She held my hand, which was in a sling.

Anna whispered, "You caught some type of virus that the doctors have never seen. They don't know how to treat you, so you are here for observations until they can figure it out. Your lungs failed after you blacked out. The doctors are running tests to find out what is wrong. You were on your way to cardiac arrest when we arrived."

I motioned for something to write on. I needed to ask some questions, and I couldn't talk. It was a bit difficult, but I managed. Anna went to the nurse's station and got me a pad of paper and a pen. The doctor came in and checked my vitals before I could write anything down.

"You are very lucky Mr. Henderson that you had someone to drive you here. I believe you would have died earlier in the day if any more time had elapsed before you arrived. You seem to be doing better now, so we will continue to monitor you and keep you up-to-date on what we figure out. I will leave you two alone for now." The doctor promptly exited the room.

I started writing questions down on the paper. I asked what happened earlier in the day.

"You went out for a jog and slipped on some ice." Anna told me. "You were running from a loose dog in the neighborhood."

I chuckled a little bit while I listened to the story, but even my laughter was gurgled as it made its way out of my throat. It was so far-fetched, and yet I remember something else; something totally different.

I wrote a question about last night at the comedy club.

"You were a different person when you got to the car." Anna calmly stated. "It should have clicked in my head when we first got here. You must have started to get sick last night. Maybe it was something you ate at Edelweiss? I told the doctors, but they don't think it is food poisoning. What I don't get is why they didn't see anything yesterday when they x-rayed your arm. They checked your vitals then, and you seemed to be as healthy as can be. I think we should contact a lawyer."

I wrote, "We have enough money."

I was more grateful to finally have answers to my insanity questions. I kept writing down my thoughts to her and that there was not going to be any frivolous lawsuits. These things happen, I mean who is really to blame, the doctor, or me for not living my life healthier. I have to take some of the blame. After the particulars of the situation had been discussed, she surprised me.

"I have never been more satisfied in bed since I had met you. You were great last night. I love you with all my heart."

I felt a little queasy at that moment because I didn't remember having sex with my wife the night before. I started to write down what was happening to me, and then I reconsidered it. I knew that it would not be something I could put into words. Hell, if I was a writer, then I wouldn't have needed to tell someone else to write my story, I would just do it. As fate has it, I am not a writer, so I left it alone at the time and waited for a better time to tell my wife what I believed was happening to me. The only problem at that point was now I knew it was not true. Everything happening to me could be rationalized as hallucinations. Just for the record, I am truly an idiot.

I finally asked for the time.

Anna told me "It is 11:45 PM."

That was probably the best news I had heard all day, except for the virus/fever part. The day was almost over, and even though I was in a hospital emergency room, I felt like a billion dollars.

Anna held my hand for a long time. We didn't communicate; we just stared at one another.

The doctor came in and told us, "We are moving you to your own room."

When all the re-situating was taken care of, they removed the ventilator from my throat and I was exhausted.

Anna told me before she left for the night, "I will be back first thing in the morning." She kissed me goodbye and left the room.

I looked outside into the dark night sky and tried to fall asleep. I couldn't really move with the I.V. and the sling on one arm. I couldn't fall asleep, so I rolled out of the bed. The really cool thing was there were no mirrors that I could see. I rolled my I.V. over to my box of clothes that the security office had delivered to my room.

I started sifting through my pants pockets. I found the piece of paper that would give me even more peace of mind. I held it up in the dim light that the outside sky reflected on the room. It was the receipt from the bank. The numbers hadn't changed. It said I was broke, and that I really was somewhere else earlier. That was my proof that I was not and am not crazy. I kind of wish the story could end here, but there really is no way for me to destroy all the mirrors in the world. Trust me, I have thought about it regularly for years.

CHAPTER 4

The ringing phone woke me up the next morning. I opened my eyes and realized I was still in the hospital. The dreams I had throughout the night gave me a queasy feeling in my stomach. I reached over and lifted the receiver to stop the ringing.

"Hello." I mumbled.

"Good morning, dear, do you need anything? I am leaving the house and wanted to check before I come to see you." Anna's voice echoed into my ear.

I tried to think but I was still half asleep. Finally, I remembered I did want to know about one thing in particular.

"Yes, stop at the bank and get me a receipt of our accounts." I stated. I was becoming more and more coherent with every second.

"Why are you always interested in money?" She bellowed back.

"Please dear, just get me the receipt. This is not about what you think it is."

I know she was leading into something else, but I was not going to feed the fire.

"Alright, well maybe I will actually listen to what this *is* about this time. You can fill me in when I get to the hospital."

"Thank you, darlin'."

"Love you." Anna said.

"I love you too." I replied and I put the receiver back on the base of the phone.

Normally I would be fixing myself a nice pot of fresh coffee at this time of the morning. However, I was stuck in the position of being at the beck and call of the hospital staff.

"Are you ready for your breakfast?" The nurse quietly said as she came into my room.

I was starving so I did not hesitate to give her my approval.

"Could you make the coffee as strong as possible?" I asked.

I was expecting it to be weak. I knew where I was and I figured the hospital coffee was brewed in bulk. Anything that is produced in bulk loses its appeal to me. Not to mention, the taste of the coffee would probably be absolutely nil. So, with that one request, I waited to see the results, knowing full well what those results would be.

I found the control pad for the bed. One thing about hospital beds is the great comfort you can find. If you find the perfect upright position, it is heavenly. The downside is it is a considerable amount of money to go to the hospital. The sick thing is, that I was in my own room, but also that I visited the E.R. twice the day before. I felt like I should use the amenities to at least get my money's worth.

Of course, I can only recall the second time, but I will take it on faith that I was there earlier. The staff and my wife tell me this is true, but when you cannot remember where you have been, have you really been there?

The nurse came back in the room and said, "It will be about fifteen minutes for your food to arrive."

I gave her a nod as a thank you and I jumped out of bed to wash up. I was headed for the bathroom, and then I realized, that I wanted to eat, which meant no mirrors! I buzzed the nurse's station.

"Could you hang a sheet over the bathroom mirror?" I asked as soon as I saw her entering the room.

She looked confused and then said, "You look fine. There is no need to hide your face."

I told her, "I don't want to see myself this morning. If you can help me with this one small favor, I promise I will not bug you for the rest of the day."

"Fine." As she left the room and came back a few minutes later with a sheet. She went into the bathroom. "It is done."

I hurried into the bathroom to clean up. I looked at the sheet hanging over the mirror, and laughed to myself. The length I was going to not see myself was becoming quite extreme. I washed up with my one good arm. It was quite the sight I am sure from an outsider's perspective. I wobbled back to my bed and waited for my breakfast.

There was a knock at the door, and then it opened. A fresh face I had not seen yet carried in my breakfast tray.

"Here is your five-star breakfast." The intern shouted jubilantly.

I think he was trying to get a laugh out of me. However, I was in no mood for humor, I already knew the breakfast was going to be horrible and so did he, his enthusiasm was a tad over the top. He set the tray down after I didn't give him a response. He left me alone to enjoy my misery, bite-by-bite.

The breakfast was sitting in front of me. I looked at the oatmeal, and trust me it was not very appealing. Then I looked at the coffee cup. It was one of those small plastic cups. I pulled off the plastic top they put on it to keep it from spilling. I put the cup up to my nose and smelled the aroma. It was horrid. I thought of the colored water I spoke about earlier.

I tried the coffee, the only similarity it had to coffee was that it was hot. Other than that, it was just colored water with heat, which might I add was probably decaffeinated. The orderly didn't say if it was and I forgot to ask. I sipped on my coffee, ate my toast, which was the only edible thing on the tray, and laid back. I didn't know how long I would have to stay in the hospital, but I was already concocting my escape plan for the nearest gourmet coffee house.

The nurse came back in and took my tray.

She told me, "The doctor will be in to see you shortly. He has just started his rounds on the floor, but he started on the other side of the wing. You are not a priority because you are obviously recuperating very fast."

I took that as a compliment, and envisioned my release from this anti-caffeine asylum. In other words, I thought about lying about my splitting headache, and body pains. The quicker I exited the hospital meant the quicker I could change my I.V. from life giving fluids to intravenous caffeine injections.

The doctor arrived shortly afterward and he had a very happy attitude.

He asked me, "How are you?"

I told him, "I am feeling great."

I was trying not to squint, but the pain in my head was forcing me too. I was hoping he wouldn't notice, because I wanted out of there. I felt like a convict who was facing the parole board. Yes, I have been rehabilitated, and no I don't think about being a bad person anymore, and yes, I have realized my mistakes harms others and myself, and no, I do not want to be a menace to society, and yes, I have plans to make myself an integral part of society. That's my impression of trying to be freed by forces holding you down.

The doctor checked my vitals.

I asked, "Am I going to be able to go home today?"

He told me the bad news right away. It really wasn't *bad,* per se, but it was bad to me.

He said, "I want to keep you in the hospital for one more night. Viral infections have a tendency to come back. I don't want my insurance rates to go up from a malpractice suit."

He tried to make me laugh by saying he didn't want his insurance rates to go up, but I didn't find it funny. Maybe it had something to do with him just telling me I was denied parole for today. He finished marking up my chart with his medical non-sense, and as he was walking out the door, I asked him, "Could I could get some aspirin?"

He asked me, "What is wrong?"

Realizing that I just lied to him about feeling great, I looked away and said, "I have a headache."

He must have realized that I felt a little guilty, but I only lied because I wanted to go home.

He told me, "I will send a nurse in with something for your headache." He then left the room for what I assumed to be finishing his rounds.

The nurse came in about ten minutes later with a small glass of water, and a mini paper cup with two tablets of aspirin in it. I tossed them into my mouth and swallowed them. She left without saying a word, and I didn't mind because I was still a little angry. I did not want to be there, and I gazed out the window. I watched the clouds float by my window off into the eastern sky.

I don't think I told you what hospital I was at, but the name of it was Our Lady of the Resurrection. It was on Central and Addison. It is a busy intersection, and I really enjoyed being on the third floor of the hospital. I was able to see the traffic below my window on Central Avenue.

I waited for my wife to arrive and to pass the time, I counted cars, and then I got bored. So, I started timing the light at the intersection. I found it funny that the green light for the Central traffic was longer than the green light for the Addison traffic. Yet, it seemed like there was more traffic heading west on Addison, than the north and south traffic on Central combined. Welcome to the City of Chicago. It is called the city that works, or the city with big shoulders, or The Windy City, as most of you already know, but I like to think it is the city where political clout gets you rich and locked up; all in the same year.

After about an hour of window gazing, my headache finally

subsided. I was very grateful for that. I guess the combination of the aspirin and the wandering mind was a good thing. My room door swung open, and there was Anna with an armful of flowers, balloons, and a card. The balloons bounced off one another as she approached my bed with a big smile.

She asked, "How is my favorite husband?"

I just laughed at her. She could get very corny at times. The balloons said "Get Well Soon". I opened the card and read the nice little Hallmark saying.

Anna put the balloons off to the side, and put the flowers on my nightstand. I thanked her for the card with a big kiss and hug. Even though it was a one-armed hug, it still worked. When she separated from the embrace, I noticed tears were forming in her eyes.

I told her; "You must have heard about me having to stay for another night?" That made her laugh. I never liked to see my wife cry, so I always used humor to lighten the load.

Anna told me, "I talked to the nurse and you shouldn't be upset because they just want to be sure you will not get any worse."

I know that is the hospital's priority, they are in the people healing business, and the dying business is for a morgue or cemetery. She sat down on my bed and I rubbed her back while we talked for a while. I think it was our first real conversation about nothing, well at least one I was interested in. I forgot all about the broken arm, and the I.V. and the mirrors. The time went by rather fast, and Anna realized the sun was beginning to set.

She told me, "You should get some rest, and the faster that you fall asleep then the faster tomorrow will come."

I couldn't agree more. She gave me a hug goodbye and a nice wet kiss. The kiss was so juicy; I had to wipe my lips with my forearm. I am sure you know the kind of kiss I am talking about; where the saliva is spread all over your cheeks and down your chin. You don't realize how messy kissing is, unless you are so into it that you forget about everything else. When I forget about the rest of the world that means I am really enjoying something. The rose-colored glasses were definitely on my face at that moment.

Just for the record, I should have forgotten about the rest of the world. If I had then maybe Anna and I would still be together today. I like to think that maybe in the next life I will have a better understanding about life, and hopefully I can find her again and not screw it up. I mean I believe in re-incarnation. I also believe that this is some sort of hell. I have to do it over and over again until I get it right. When I finally do get it right then maybe I can move up the ladder to the next level of life.

It is similar to the beliefs of Buddhism, but I like to think I have cornered the market on the God/Heaven/Devil/Hell theory. Maybe I will go into it in more detail later on. I want to get back to the story now, because I think you will be very interested in the next turn of events.

I almost forgot something else because of that kiss, but I remembered as Anna was walking out the room.

"Anna," I yelped her name.

She turned to me wondering why I was so unruly.

"What about the receipt?" I asked.

She giggled to herself, and reached into her purse for it. She pulled it out and began to walk over to me.

"I hoped you had forgotten about it." She told me. "Money should not be your main motivation in life."

I knew she was implying that she should be my main focus, but the receipt had nothing to do with my daily money-making routine. This was different because of where I had been. I needed to know how different the other side of the mirror really was.

"Thanks again babe. You are so much more important to me than our money, or all the money in the world for that matter."

It made her smile, and then she said, "I will see you tomorrow."

I just nodded and waited for the door to close behind her. I knew she would be waiting for me to look at the receipt. However, I am a pretty sly fox. I didn't even look away from her until I heard the door latch.

I picked up the receipt off of my lap. It said I had eighty-six thousand dollars in my savings and fourteen thousand in my checking. Now, sure you probably think that is a good amount of money. I didn't think so. I was short almost five thousand from my savings and five thousand from my checking. I know my wife would have told me if she spent ten thousand dollars, but I was starting to get the feeling like it wasn't my wife who spent the money.

I grabbed the other receipt from my nightstand drawer. I compared the account numbers. Now, the account numbers are usually blocked out except for the last four digits. The numbers were the same, but the amounts were quite different. I put the receipts down on my lap and laid my head back for a minute to think about where my money had gone.

I knew if I asked my wife about it, it would just cause an argument. I figured I would just do some investigating myself. It was Sunday, so I knew the bank was closed, but I had to get out of the hospital tomorrow in order to find out what had happened. I also knew I had better call my broker first thing tomorrow to make sure there was nothing wrong with my accounts at his firm.

Thinking about all the possibilities was causing my head to start hurting again. Identity theft was one thought I had. I know identity thieves can access accounts and they don't steal all your money right away, they do it in sections. It is kind of like cutting a pie. You start by cutting the whole pie in half, then into quarters and finally into pieces. Then you remove piece by piece. Identity thieves work the same way. They begin to cut your pie into pieces, and then 'take a piece of your pie'.

I must have dozed off, because I don't remember the nurse coming

45

into my room. I awoke to her touching my arm with the I.V. I was startled for a second, and then I realized that she was removing the I.V. That made me happy. When the medical equipment begins to disappear, it means you are one step closer to getting out the hospital.

I was kind of groggy from my little catnap. I was not asleep very long, because the sun was barely finished setting. She turned the light on above my head.

"Dinner will be here shortly." She said. "Do you want your sheets changed?"

"Sure, that would be nice."

Plus, it gave me a reason to get up and wash up. I had that bad taste in my mouth. I always called it the morning after taste. I needed to brush my teeth and wash my face. I came out of the bathroom and they had already finished making my bed.

I ran over to the bed and realized I had forgotten about my receipts. I started throwing things around, looking for where I might have put them. Then I remembered they were on my lap when I fell asleep. I sprinted for the door. I opened the door and ran out into the hallway. My hospital gown was flapping in the wind, but I didn't care what the nurses or patients saw. Those receipts were my proof that something stranger than a virus was happening to me. I raced over to the nurse's station.

I asked, "Where are the laundry bins from the used sheets that are on this wing?"

The nurse on duty told me, "They have just taken it down to the laundry."

"I had my bank receipts on the bed, I thought I had them on my lap or in my nightstand, but I am certain they were on the bed. I need those receipts. It is so important..." The phone began to ring.

She looked at the phone, and then at me. She was obviously hinting to me that she was going to answer the phone, and put me on hold.

I looked up and down the corridor and then I saw the elevator.

I bolted down the corridor to it. I noticed as I was running towards the elevator that the doors were made of stainless steel. I was looking at myself as I neared the doors. I ran and pushed the down button, which is where I assumed the laundry room would be. I stood there looking up at the numbers above the door. The elevator was in the basement.

I took a quick glance back down the corridor towards the nurses' station, and didn't see anybody. I turned back around and looked at my reflection in the elevator doors. I blinked and then I saw two of me. I looked to my right and saw my reflection was standing next to me. A couple seconds passed, and then he was gone. I looked around the wing and nothing seemed to be out of place.

I looked up at the elevator lights above the doors, and it was still in the basement. I tried to push the down button again, but this time it would not light up. I waited for a few seconds and then returned to the nurses' station. She was off of the phone.

I asked, "Are the elevators broken?"

"They are locked!"

Locked I thought, why would it be locked?

"Why would the elevators be locked?" I asked.

"It is a secure wing." She told me. "This is the rehabilitation unit, and nobody is allowed to leave without the doctor's permission."

I was confused, and she could tell by the look on my face.

I told her, "I was not on the rehabilitation wing."

She stood up and walked around her counter towards me. She held my arm.

"It is okay sir. You are going to be okay."

I didn't understand, and then she guided me by my arm back to my room.

She sat me down on the bed, "Dinner will be here soon. That should make you feel better." She walked out of the room, and shut the door behind her.

After a few seconds of thinking, I jumped up and ran back to the door. The door was locked. I started pounding on the door.

"Let me out of here."

"Hello, can you hear me, let me out!" I must have been pounding for a few minutes, and yet nobody came to my calls. Finally, I was so frustrated I wandered back to the window and realized there were steel panels over the windows.

This is when I realized my reflection had got me again. I ran into the bathroom. I saw the sheet over the mirror, and pulled it down. There I was standing on the other side. I put my hands up to the mirror and tried to figure out how to switch places with myself. I started pounding on the glass, and then finally; it broke.

I looked at myself through the shattered mirror. A crack had formed from the spider web of my fist; it went from the left of the mirror to the right. I was going crazy, and there was nothing I could do about it.

I fell to my knees and started crying out, "Why are you doing this to me?" My reflection mimicked me, like some kind of game. I crawled out of the bathroom, with my one arm. I left a trail of blood from my busted fist. I finally collapsed on the floor of room, and just stared at the ceiling.

I heard the click from the lock on the door. The door swung open and two interns rushed in and grabbed me. The put me in my bed and strapped me down with arm and leg restraints. I tried to fight the restraints but I was not strong enough. Just another experience I was having for the first time. Let me tell you that would not be the last time I experienced something new.

A nurse came into the room and pulled up a chair next to my bed. She looked at my cut fist and pulled a few remaining pieces of mirror out of the cuts. She started to swab the wound with something that burned my skin. She saw my discomfort and then started blowing on the cuts. She bandaged up my hand and was about to leave, but I realized that might have been my only chance to ask some questions. Rather than think about it, I just opened my mouth and hoped the right words were going to come out.

I asked, "How long do I have to stay restrained?"

She told me, "I will send the doctor in as soon as possible."

"How long have I been in the hospital?" I asked.

She looked at me with a puzzled look. Then she must have realized that I was serious.

"Sir, you signed yourself in yesterday. You asked to be put into this detoxification facility. The observation period for heroin withdrawal is a minimum three days."

This was something I never knew. I guess I really didn't care to know, but I was beginning to understand my reflection's lifestyle. I mean heroin withdrawal; I couldn't believe those two words put together could even describe my personality.

It seems I was a junkie. At least, this is what I assumed. I recalled the bathroom incident from a few days earlier and then the mark on my arm. This really messed with my head, because how does one thing happen to my reflection, yet a totally different circumstance happens to me. I was restrained for hours while I tossed around these crazy ideas in my head. Throughout my thinking process I began to formulate what had been happening to me. I started at the beginning and then worked my way through the events of the last three days. I ended up with a ton of questions, and very few answers. This was becoming a regular theme.

The questions I asked myself ran along the lines of, how did I get back? Why was I always sleeping whenever I returned to my reality? Was this even reality? How does my reflection control the switching of places with me? Where is my wife in this world? How long do I have to be restrained? Is this going to be happening to me for rest of my life? Is there medication for this? Finally, the doctor arrived, right after I was asking myself about the medication.

"Hello Mr. Henderson. I am going to ask you some questions. Is that okay?" The doctor stated in a condescending tone.

"Yes."

"What are your inner feelings at this moment? What emotions are you feeling?" He asked in a calm. low volume tone.

"I don't know doctor. I am exhausted."

"Are you having any withdrawal symptoms, such as knots in your abdomen, or hot or cold flashes?"

I had no idea what withdrawal symptoms from heroin were even like. I told him, "I feel fine." I did except for the fractured arm, cuts on my hand, massive headache from no caffeine, and everything else that had happened to me in the past 72 hours.

"You are supposed to be released on Tuesday. Why did you smash the mirror in your bathroom?"

"I am tired of looking at myself."

"You will begin to like yourself in the future and hopefully even love yourself. That is when the real healing begins for alcoholics and addicts."

I guess self-loathing is a common factor for drug addicts. Again, there was so much information that I did not know about, it was becoming quite the task to keep up. I finally realized I needed to get out of the hospital, which meant I needed to make this doctor see that there was no drug problem.

"I am going to remove the restraints."

That is when I had a moment of clarity.

"We will keep you unrestrained as long as you acknowledge that me and my staff are here to help you. You are not to participate in any more self-destructive behaviors either. Are these agreeable terms?"

My answer was a no-brainer, "Yes, I agree." I then blew that doctor's mind.

"Doc, could you drug test me?"

The doctor look very confused, he knew they had already done a test on me when I supposedly arrived yesterday.

"I want to be tested again, and my deal is if I am clean, I should be released.

The doctor said, "I don't make deals with patients on their terms."

I got really smart and asked, "How can a man be held in a drug rehab if he has no drugs in his system?"

It must have convinced him to have another test administered because he said, "I will send in the nurse to take a urine test."

He went out into the hallway and a nurse came back in with the same two interns who strapped me down.

"Are you going to cause any more trouble after we remove the restraints?" They asked.

This was a stupid question, because I would lie if I was going to cause trouble. They took off the straps, and I sat up. The interns stood there for a second while the nurse helped me put my sling back on my busted arm.

She helped me up out of the bed and escorted me to the bathroom. At first, she handed me a cup for my urine, then stopped and realized there was still broken glass all over the floor in the bathroom. She took me out into the hallway to use the bathroom on the wing. I went into the bathroom and looked at myself.

I smiled really cocky, because I was finally getting the hang of this game. I pointed to myself and laughed because I was about to get over on my reflection for once. Yeah, I know you think I am crazy, but just wait and see how crazy a sane man gets when he finds true reality.

I handed the cup back to the nurse and she dipped an instant drug test into my urine. I never even knew they had such a thing. I always thought when you applied for jobs and you had to go in for drug testing that it had to be sent out to a lab. Now they have these fancy little pocket testers. I mean these things can fit in the palm of your hand. They come with a little eyedropper and everything included. It only takes two drops and seven minutes later you have your results.

Negative across the board was what came back. What I mean is, I had nothing in my system that those tests look for. I felt really good inside, because I knew they were going to set me free. I didn't care what papers I signed to get in; I was now envisioning signing papers to get out.

"Go back to your room while I get the doctor." The nurse said.

I found my clothes hanging in the closet. I got dressed and sat on my bed. I looked at myself, and there I was with a sling on my left arm, my right hand was wrapped in gauze, and I all I could do was laugh. The doctor came in about ten minutes later with a clipboard full of new paperwork.

I asked him, "What do all these papers mean?"

"If you are leaving you have to sign papers saying you are refusing medical treatment. I recommend you stay; therefore, you must sign a refusal form for the facility to release you. The results say you have no drugs in your system, therefore I have no authority to keep you here."

"Thanks doc. I told you this has all been a confusing ordeal. I don't know what made me come here yesterday. Thanks for your help, I really appreciate it." I was trying to ease his mind, since he had gone out of his way to fix my problem. I felt a little guilty that I coaxed him into doing it through logic and reason.

I signed all the papers on the clipboard. They were not that hard to understand. It all made sense and was exactly how the doctor explained it.

"Good luck to you Mr. Henderson."

"Thanks again doc."

"Just remember if you need help, we are here to help."

I walked out of my hospital room and headed for the elevator, again. As I approached the stainless-steel doors, I eyed myself carefully. I didn't have any idea what to expect any more whenever I was looking at myself. I approached the elevator and tried the button again. I looked up at the numbers above the door, and it still wasn't stopping at my floor.

I looked over my shoulder, and then turned back to the elevator. Finally, I gave up and headed back to the nurse's station. I told her I would like to be let out of this place. Well, I said it a little differently and with a not so nice tone, but I don't want to be vulgar while I tell you the story. Just think of that guy who cuts you off while you are driving, and then flicks you off like it is your fault. I was that guy that night.

She stopped what she was doing and huffed out a sigh. She pushed herself out of her chair using her desk for support. I could tell she was trying to express to me her discontent with *me*. I followed her back to the elevator. I watched the elevator's numbers finally reach my floor. The doors opened and she headed back to her busy job. I mean she was obviously overworked. I am being sarcastic, but how much work can an overpaid babysitter working the graveyard shift actually have in a detoxification unit?

I walked into the elevator and the doors shut in front of me. I stared at myself really hard. This is when I began to think about getting even with myself. If he was enjoying my life, then why shouldn't I start to enjoy his? I pressed the lobby button on the console and the elevator headed down. I exited the elevator and didn't want to give myself the satisfaction of a second look.

I headed for the front doors. It looked cold outside, but I didn't care because I was feeling really good. I had talked my way out of the hospital after all. I couldn't do it earlier on my side, and then I started thinking how the other side of the mirror was playing out. If I was leaving the hospital then my reflection was leaving the hospital. That question bothered me for a second, but I shrugged it off and headed outside.

I was smiling from ear to ear. I felt like I had just taken on Patton and his army of tanks in the desert by myself. Unlike Rommel, I was victorious. This was becoming quite the battle of wits between me and me, except I wasn't very happy when I realized that I was not wearing warm enough clothes for the cold Chicago night. I opened my wallet and saw that I still had hundreds. I started to think about calling a cab then as the idea grew in my head; I went back inside the hospital to follow through with that thought. I really didn't have anywhere in particular to go, but wherever I was going; I definitely was going to need a ride to get there.

While I sat there waiting for my cab to show up, I started to realize where all my money had gone. My reflection must have withdrawn the money yesterday. It was all becoming clear. I was stealing from myself. Now you are probably thinking to yourself how crazy I am. I just want to clarify that I started thinking of my reflection as a separate person. Sure, you are laughing at me, but it really is not that funny. How long would you allow yourself to steal from you? I worked hard for my money, and I wasn't going to just let someone steal it from me. Even if it was me doing the stealing, okay, that sounded bad.

My cab arrived and I jumped in. The cabbie turned around and asked me where I was going. The funny thing is that his guess was as good as mine. I told him to give me a second while I thought about where I needed to go. It was Sunday night and it was really late. I looked at the clock on the dashboard it read 12:20 AM. It had been a long time since I spent a late night without my wife. I told the cabbie I wanted to go to the strip club. He asked me if I had one in particular, I wanted to go too. I said no, and he told me he knew just the place.

I looked out the window as we headed for Crazy Horse II. I figured since this wasn't my world, I might as well act like I don't belong here. I mean I was with my wife, or my reflection was for that matter. Then I finally realized what he meant when we first met. He told me he enjoyed living my life that first night. I thought to myself, what a son of a bitch. Then I realized I just called my mother a bitch. It was becoming really confusing for me, since I had just called my own mother a bitch.

My brain kept second-guessing every word, phrase, every action, movement, and thought to the point of eye-splitting pain. When I was about to ask to use the cab driver's mirror, I realized we had arrived. I gave up trying to look at myself, and took the next five minutes trying to pull my wallet out and pay for the ride. My one hand was all bandaged, and the other was in a sling.

I finally paid my fare and jumped out. The night air was crisp, and the cabbie threw me his card and told me to call him when I was through. He would come back and pick me up. I thought that was mighty cool of him, and then realized that is the business of a cab driver. Keep your fares happy, and they will return with more business.

I was becoming more and more naïve the longer I was out of the business world. I still would love to think that people care for me because I am a good person. The truth is that money makes everyone's decisions. I started realizing that money was my main motivation. I got to thinking about how I could change that about my personality. Then, I realized that would probably take the rest of my life, so why waste the time.

I entered the dark club. There were so many beautiful women all over the room. There were also a lot of guys throughout the room spending their hard-earned money. If all the wives in the world had seen the sight, I tell you, there would have been a lot of guys at the florist the next day. I found a nice little dark spot in the corner. I wanted to stay away from the bar area. That is where all the mirrors were. I could just imagine seeing myself now.

A few girls wandered by me and none of them interested me enough to want to buy a lap dance. I waited and waited, and then this cute little blonde girl came wandering by me. She was wearing a cute little catholic schoolgirl outfit; I think you know what I mean, the high white socks to the knees, and the unbuttoned white collared shirt that was tied above her navel. Her hair was in pigtails, and she had obviously been working the room very well. She whispered in my ear, and I agreed to her request.

I pulled out the wallet, and let her pull a hundred out. It was too much work for me to pull out the money. I thought her eyes were going to come out of her head. Yeah, I had a lot of money on me, and it was all my money, I figured I might as well spend it.

Why leave it here for him to spend it, he didn't earn it, and if he did, where was it? Why was he broke? I know he must have done some of the same things. I mean there are countless times I can remember my partner and me standing in front of mirrors or reflective glass. Or when we sealed our first big account, we both stood in front of the mirror to take a picture of us holding the check. Since there was nobody else around, it was the only way for us to be in the same picture together. I was becoming more and more interested in his life. The more answers I got just tripled the amount of questions I was asking myself.

She gave me a great lap dance, and I was turned on considerably. Now don't get me wrong, I am a guy, so turning me on is really not that hard. I had a few beers, and looked around the room for the bathroom. I began stumbling through the rather large room. Wherever I went there were beautiful women dancing for money. I giggled to myself because my wife would have killed me if she saw me here.

Eventually I found the bathroom, stumbled in, and looked at myself in the mirror as I passed the sink on the way to the urinal. I was feeling pretty buzzed, so I figured it was time I tried to call the cabbie and head back to the Esquire. I knew that is where I was staying. I didn't have the room key, but they knew me, or at least they knew my reflection.

I finished my business in the bathroom, and headed for the sink to wash my hands. The door swung open behind me. I glanced up at the mirror, and then at the beautiful women who entered behind me. I almost threw up right there in the sink. There she was, standing behind me putting her hands up and down my chest. Now, you are probably thinking it was that cute blonde; well, you are wrong. It was my wife, Anna.

She was dressed up in a really sexy outfit. I didn't know how to react. I mean was I busted? Had my delusions finally stopped? Was this real? Again, the brain began an. onslaught of questions. I tried to talk, but she put her fingers up to her mouth in a sexy fashion. I understood to stay quiet, and I wanted to stay quiet anyway. She began to unbutton my pants. She was using the mirror as her guide. I looked down at my pants, and then up at myself. I smiled like a high school kid who was about to lose his virginity.

She pulled me away from the mirror and threw me into one of the stalls. She sat me down on the toilet and began to touch herself all sexy-like. Now you probably want me to finish this story for you. However, I can really only account for bits and pieces of what happened next. I have numerous memories of that stall, but they are all visual memories. When I say visual, I mean visual, I am sure you will see why in a second.

That is when my head started to spin. I remember feeling a warm feeling in the base of my neck and then it traveled up into my head. I watched my eyes fade in and out of blackness. Whenever I could focus, I watched as Anna lifted my wallet. I faded out again, and when I came too, I saw Anna stuffing my whole wad of cash into her bra.

That is when I realized I couldn't move my arms. They felt so heavy, like there were weights attached to my wrists. I am sure it didn't help that I was pretty beat up. I really wasn't in any condition to fight her off. Not that I was thinking about fighting back.

I felt really good. I almost didn't care that she was stealing all of my money. That is when I started laughing uncontrollably. She gave me a weird look and then ran out of the stall. She left me there, and I realized I had been drugged. Whatever it was, it felt great, but I had the craziest feeling that I would not like it in the morning.

I do want you to know that these events might sound really crazy, but I found them to be quite what the doctored ordered. I was being robbed of my sanity, money, and personality day in and day out. The craziest thing about it is that I never felt so alive. I was becoming a different person with every passing moment, and yet I was still living my life.

Well, in a sense it was my life, but I was beginning to enjoy this other side of the mirror a hell of a lot more than my boring side. Maybe this was just a psychotic episode I have concocted to make myself change. This would be a great explanation, but I know it is not the truth. I have sat on this story for many years. It has taken a lot of courage on my part to even sit here and tell the story to you. I have made sure that every word I say is the truth. I feel if I do not speak the truth then the story is just as meaningless to me as it would be to you. I have run it in my head over and over, but dreams do not make you break arms. Dreams also do not cut your fists, empty your bank accounts, or allow others to sleep with your wife. Well, I am getting a little overworked now, give me a second here and let me collect my thoughts. I was going somewhere with this before I got sidetracked...

Okay, this is how I remember those days, and I want you to understand everything completely before I continue on. I know I just stopped in the middle of my story, but I want to make sure you are following along; okay? I had been switching places with myself through mirrors.

Although, I didn't realize it fully until I was drugged. I understood why my reflection had chosen the path of drugs. It was a great feeling in my body to be under the influence of something besides alcohol. I felt alive, and yet I couldn't move. I will not try to explain this further, because I still do not believe in the whole drug scene, even to this day. I am going to take you back to the story now because I think my explanations are probably confusing you.

As you can imagine, there I was perched on a toilet in a strip club. All my money had just been taken by my wife, my arm was in a sling, the other hand was all bandaged up, my fly was unbuttoned, and luckily, I was slumped up against the wall, because I don't think I would have been able to pick myself up from the floor if I fell.

I must have been on that toilet for a long time, because I can remember a lot. The drugs I had been given only affected my brain's reactions. It didn't affect my memory. I finally passed out. What time was it? I have no idea. I just remember fading out into a really peaceful sleep. It was also the first time that I was on this side of the mirror and my last memory of the day was not painful. If only I could stay so lucky.

CHAPTER 5

11:38 AM was the time on the clock. It had been a long time since I slept that late. My head was pounding, and my body ached all over. I looked over and saw that my wife was not in the bed. I was lying there staring at the ceiling. I thought about the night before. I still had that feeling that nothing was real. I was becoming more and more worried about my psychotic episodes. I needed to talk to someone. I knew I should have told the doctor yesterday, but I wanted out of the hospital, not permanently admitted. It felt so real, whenever I was on the other side, I felt like I was living a whole different life. Honestly, I was starting to enjoy the break from my boredom.

I was starting to figure out how I would always end up in my world whenever I woke up. Every time I would fall asleep on the other side, I would wake up and everything would be normal on this side. I started wondering if that is how I could control it. Maybe if I could force myself asleep then I would be able to combat my reflection's control over switching spots. Now, these were the things I was thinking about lying there in bed. I know it all sounds crazy, but how would you react to something like this. Would you run and tell someone? Or would you wait and try to fix it yourself? I think you would wait, just like I had been. I mean nobody wants to tell others that they think they are crazy. People do not respond well to those conversations.

I was beginning to feel a little guilty about the lap dances. I mean was I cheating on my wife. The guilt started out as a small sensation in the back of my head. Then it gained momentum the longer I was lying there staring at the ceiling. Finally, I pushed that part out of my thoughts for a minute. I needed to combat this somehow. I also needed to talk to Anna about it. I figured before I ran off to some psychiatrist about my mirror episodes, maybe I had better run it by my life partner. At least I knew she was sane. I also found it funny that she didn't notice my disappearing acts.

I rolled over onto her side of the bed, and then buried my face in her pillow. I loved the way my wife smelled. I had my face buried for a few minutes while I ran the conversation, I needed to have with her in my mind. I figured I would sit her down, and then try and explain about my memory lapses. I knew that telling her the whole story would come out wrong. I would start to tell her about the first time I lost my mind. I was brushing my teeth and I started hearing the knocking. Yet nobody was at the door. Then I would wait for her reaction, and if it brought on a smile then I could continue.

If the reaction were a plain look, then I would stop telling her every detail and just tell her I have been zoning out mentally, yet it would look like nothing is wrong. I stopped thinking about that, because if that happened, I would have to explain it differently. I thought again about explaining it differently. I would have to spend a lot of time thinking about this. As I rolled my face out of her pillow and returned to staring at the ceiling. I swung my feet over the side of the bed and stared out the window. It was sunny out, and the weather outside still looked cold, but the sun was shining, so it could not have been that bad out there.

I looked at my broken arm and tried to stretch out my shoulder. Finally, I got tired of looking at the sling, and took it off. I threw it in the corner of the room. It flew into the wall and slid down into the crevasse the dresser and the wall made. I started stretching my shoulder out. I mean my arm was fractured, not broken. There was need for a cast; therefore, there was no need for a sling. I looked at my bandaged hand and started unraveling the gauze. I turned my wrist upwards so I could see the backside of my fist. The cuts still looked fresh, but scabs had formed, so that was just another thing I didn't need medical attention for. My headache had subsided. I stood up from the bed and looked at the clock. 12:07 PM that made me feel good. I had made it through the day before without too much caffeine.

I would have normally rolled right out of bed and made myself a pot of coffee. But I didn't feel like drinking coffee today. I looked at my slippers on the floor, and then I realized that they did look girly. I put my right foot in the slipper, lifted it up to my hand, grabbed it off my foot, and tossed it into the open closet door. I stuffed the other one under the bed with my other foot. I was getting tired of my routine. I reached over and pushed my robe off of the foot of bed.

As you can tell I was becoming complacent. I was getting irritated because of the whole ordeal. I was beginning to really dislike myself. When I say that; I am talking about both of me. My reflection was a junkie, and I was just a bored man looking for a way out. The future looked unbearable. The decisions I was faced with were becoming headaches. I didn't know what I was doing or where I was going. I was becoming paranoid with any shiny or reflective surface. Now that I think about it; I was starting to become the worst type of man, one with nothing to lose.

I have a theory about a man who has nothing to lose. The man will do or say anything that will help him. Like a wolverine that gets cornered will attack fiercely because it knows it is either do or die. The same holds true for a man. This man I speak of was becoming me. The thoughts that were running through my head on that day were like a wolverine's thoughts. Was my reflection trying to take my life away from me? Was he trying to take my wife from me? He was obviously taking my money and who knows what else. So, I started to do some serious thinking on investigating me from the inside out. I decided the best way for that was to write down all my dreams, fears, irrational thoughts, et cetera, and then I would break it all down and try to figure out the likenesses between myself and I.

I walked out into the kitchen, and saw there was a fresh pot of coffee already made. Anna must have brewed it up. I called out her name, and after hearing no response I realized that she must have gone somewhere. I turned off the coffee maker. Then I grabbed the full pot and walked over to the sink. I tipped the pot over the sink and watched as my caffeine dreams swirled down the drain. I ran the water and rinsed out the pot. The one thing I hated about other people and coffee is that they never wash out the pot after the last cup. I don't understand this, the only result that happens is a stained pot, and of course a pissed of Jack.

I put the pot back into the maker and wandered over to the front room. I turned on the market, and looked at the numbers. It took me a whole twenty seconds to get irritated from the analysts talking on the Bloomberg Channel. I clicked through the channels and then finally just switched off the television. I sat there in my recliner and looked out of the sliding glass door into the backyard. The snow was still on the ground, but the reflection of the sun on the ground was a pleasant sight. I sat there for a while just daydreaming.

Finally, I rose up from my comfortable chair and headed for the bathroom to clean up. Just before I entered the bathroom, I got the strangest urge to stop. Then I decided against seeing myself in the mirror. I mean I knew what I looked like. I had a beard that was a week old. My face was covered in freckles, my hair was red, and I felt irritable that day. These are things I didn't need a mirror to tell me about. Not to mention, I really didn't feel like switching places today.

I got on my hands and knees and crawled into the bathroom and reached up onto the sink for my toothbrush and the toothpaste tube. I started crawling out of the bathroom into my kitchen. That is where I started brushing my teeth. I didn't hear the garage door open because of the noise of my brushing mixed with the running water. I spit out the toothpaste into the sink, and rinsed my mouth out with two handfuls of water. I reached for the paper towel rack, and realized there were no paper towels to grab. I swore under my breath and turned around to go to the garage for a fresh roll.

I was startled when I turned to see my wife standing in the kitchen with her arms folded. She obviously had been watching me, and I shrugged my shoulders and told her we needed paper towels. She didn't say a word, instead she pointed to the kitchen table. There were three bags resting on each other for support. I looked and saw the couple rolls of paper towels that were in one of the bags. I walked over and grabbed a roll. I tore off the wrapper and threw it on the counter. I removed the rod that held the paper towels from the rack. I pulled off the spent cardboard tube and then I placed the new roll on the rod and then put it back. I turned around to see if Anna was still watching me the whole time.

There she was with that angry look plastered on her face. I shrugged my shoulders again, but this time I said, "What!" She started asking me why I was brushing my teeth in the kitchen sink. I told her I didn't feel like doing it in the bathroom today. That is when she lost it. I don't know how she was feeling but I can tell you how I felt. I was mad, why was she yelling at me. So, what, I brushed my teeth in the kitchen sink. Oh, how much of a crime is that! Really, the whole situation was ridiculous. I thought that is what it was all about, and then I realized that I was mistaken.

Anna started asking me about the night before. She insisted on me telling her why I was so adamant about leaving the hospital. She also informed me that she did not like my new style of lovemaking. She told me how she enjoyed the dress up and the role-playing, but the intimacy afterwards made her feel cheap. I started asking questions of my own. This was becoming the perfect time to lead into my changing personality theory.

I told her to sit down. I needed to tell her something but I needed her to listen to me with a serious, open mind. She pulled out her chair and sat down. I decided that maybe I should stay standing; this would assure that I would be out of arms reach from a slap in the face. I began to tell her my day's events from a few days earlier. I figured starting at the beginning with the knocks at the door that I had heard, and the changing of my attitude was a great place to start.

I didn't get the chuckle out of her liked I had hoped. The whole review process I did this morning before I got out of bed was not working in my favor. She looked very confused, and let me tell you I was probably more confused than she was. I tried to explain that I couldn't remember anything from last night. The things that I did remember were not the same things she was telling me.

She started to cry and she buried her face in her hands. Then in an instant she stood up and walked towards me. She put her hands on my face and I looked into her beautiful eyes. I could see the teardrops running down her cheeks. She whispered to me that I was crazy, and I should never again tell her I couldn't remember having sex with her. If I do say those words again to her, she will leave me without hesitation. I realized right there that I had better say something fast, because I was losing this battle.

I said to her, "Look I need to see a doctor." She stopped crying and looked into my eyes, and then she must have realized that I was being serious. I had a blank look, but I meant what I said. I needed to see a head doctor as soon as possible. She said I looked pretty serious. She told me to go lie down for a while and she would start making some phone calls. I love that woman; she always went above and beyond and that day was not any different.

The clock read 12:54 PM when I sat on the bed. I didn't mind that time was going slow that day. There obviously was a ton of things that I needed to get accomplished. I rolled into the bed on my back, and began to stare at the ceiling again. I almost thought I screwed up by telling Anna the story. It turned out all right though. I have to admit that I was a very sly fox that day. I didn't want to scare her with the other side of the mirror, but she still understood that I was losing my sanity, one moment at a time. That was the plan this morning when I woke up. I had to make Anna believe something was wrong.

I must have done a great job, because when I opened my eyes, Anna was shaking me and telling me to get dressed we were going to the doctor's office. I asked if it was at the hospital, and she said no. She had called the insurance company and was told whom she could take me too. I mean, insurance costs money, so I had better go through my primary insurance carrier. Like I said earlier, she was a great wife, and I would have probably committed suicide if she weren't around during that week before Christmas.

I got dressed and we went to the doctor. The ride to the doctor was quiet. She didn't say anything to me. I also didn't feel like saying much anyway. I watched the scenery as we headed down Elston Avenue towards Touhy. The doctor's office was on Touhy, just west of Harlem. It was a little enclave of Chicago that was surrounded by Park Ridge and Niles.

Anna pulled into the back of the building where there was patient parking. We entered the office and I sat down in the waiting room. Anna checked me in with the receptionist, and the doctor came out to meet me within a few minutes. I followed him down the hallway to his office. It was about time to tell this story to someone who could prescribe me something to fix it. The only worry I had was there might not be any drugs to fix it, if that was the case there might be only one other solution.

I have to tell you, going to a psych ward is my biggest fear. I do not think I could handle being locked away without my wife or my life. I would have to be at the beck and call of the doctors. This made me feel queasy, but I had to push out the fears and tell this doctor everything.

He told me to have a seat in the chair. He walked around his desk and sat down. He looked over his desk at me. He asked me some personal questions, but they were obviously just to make me feel comfortable. I began to tell him about the past few days' events. His expression didn't change much, which made me feel a little crazy. By the time I finished telling him about the strip club, he had filled up a whole page on his legal pad with notes. I eyed him carefully, and then he spoke. He told me his medical opinion first.

He believed I was beginning to develop a split personality. I was creating a second me who was crazier and more carefree than myself. The whole time he was talking to me, I was reminded of the various movies I had seen. There are so many movies and books that talk about multiple personalities. I would love to say this is some form of schizophrenia, but how can it be when I remember the other side of the mirror. The world over there is similar, and yet people's lives are different than they are over here. I tried to ask about that, but the doctors only responded by prescribing me some medication. He told me to take the medication, and report back to him after Christmas. He was going on vacation on Wednesday, and wouldn't be back until next Monday. So, he wanted to see me next week.

Before I got up to leave with the new prescription, he told me he wanted to try some therapy. He rose from behind his desk and walked out of the office. He returned a few minutes later with a make-up case. He told me this was his receptionist's, and he looked through the case and found a small mirror. He handed me the mirror and told me not to open it yet. He walked back around his desk and sat down. He told me he wanted me to open the mirror and talk to myself. He was certain that I would not disappear to some other reality. I didn't want to open the mirror. I tried really hard to not see my reflection today.

On the way to the office, I would shut my eyes when I saw a storefront window. I was afraid of my reflection, and there are a lot of places where you can look at yourself besides mirrors. I sighed really hard, and then pushed that fear down in my stomach. I began to open the mirror, and I shut my eyes. When I opened them, I looked at myself? It was my reflection in the mirror, and I was waiting to switch places. That never happened. The doctor told me to do that every morning while I was on the medication. Hopefully, my brain would keep me in check. That was his theory. Of course, I have my own theories.

I was about to close the mirror, and the doctor was writing out the prescription, when I had a thought that was not my own. It was my voice in my head, but it was my reflection talking to me. I looked at the mirror and my lips were not moving. I told myself, "There is no need for this quack. We are not crazy. Look, I told you I needed your help, and you have been great so far. So let me fill you in on a few things while I have your attention." I looked up at the doctor to see if he was aware of my thoughts. He continued to write on his pad and in my new file.

"Alright, you have been living the good life for years, while I have been over here picking up the scraps. You won't understand this right away. But it will start to make sense after you think about it. When we were younger and you would look at my side of the mirror, you used to think I had a different world. Well, I do. I didn't have the loving family at home like you did. Our parents split up in my world, but they stayed together to try and raise me right. I went to college like you, but I liked partying more than you did. I started realizing that my brain was the exact opposite of yours. You always knew how to make the right choices. I always had to make the wrong ones. I have spent 30 years of my life doing almost the exact opposite of you except for a few core decisions."

I didn't understand, "I know you don't understand but let me finish, so quit thinking for a minute. Remember when you retired with all that money. Well, I retired too obviously, and yes, I had that money. I made a few bad business deals, and now I am broke. I took some money from your accounts on Saturday, so whatever you have in your pockets when you leave here stays with you and the same works for me. So, that is how I had all those hundreds, which conveniently was not here when I woke up this morning. I wouldn't have bitched, but what the fuck did you do last night? Forget it, it doesn't matter. Whoever is on your side of the mirror controls most of the good fortune. I just get your scraps. A lot of things stay the same, but a lot more are different. So, tomorrow will be the last time I bother you.

You don't need the medication; I will not be asking for any more favors either, well except for maybe asking you to screw up a few things on your end once in a while. Anyway, meet me tomorrow morning in the bathroom at 8 AM. I need you to sit in my hotel room for one day, while I take care of some things on your side. Now don't worry, I won't cause any trouble, but I need to find someone who can help me over here. If I can find this guy's reflection, then maybe I can get back on track. I know you are thinking I am the crazy one. You are right, I am the crazy one, but if you don't help me tomorrow, I will continue to fuck with you for years to come. You and I will end up in the psych ward together, which will not bother *me* one bit; besides I could probably use the vacation. 8 AM, tomorrow, be there!"

I heard the doctor call my name, and I snapped out of my trance. He asked me if I was all right. I must have had a blank stare. I told him I was fine, and that he was right, I was still here. Hearing myself tell the doctor that I was still here, made me realize that there was some sort of control here. I mean why my reflection didn't just switch places with me. Instead, he asked me for my approval this time.

I thanked the doctor, grabbed my prescription, told him I would see him next week, and then I asked if we were finished. He told me we were, and I jumped up and flew out of the office. I had to get home really fast.

I ran out into the waiting room and told Anna we had to go. She looked puzzled, and was about to say something. Then I handed her the prescription and told her I needed this filled but I needed to get home. I was feeling better, but I needed a nap. She could drop me off, and then go to the pharmacy to fill the prescription. She was obviously satisfied with that answer because she got up, grabbed her things, and followed me out to the car.

On the way home, Anna tried to get me to tell her about the visit. I told her I felt funny talking about it with her, and that was the whole reason I needed to see a doctor. She didn't like that, but she was trying to make herself be more understanding about my situation. I could see that her patience was running thin, but she was a survivor. I knew she would be okay. It was the idea of my brain not being all right.

I started to think about why my reflection would even ask me to help him. I mean, was this a ploy for me to not take my medication? Would the medication work? Maybe that was it; I was worried about losing my new personality. I rolled the ideas back and forth throughout my head and then I figured I would take a nap when I got home. This way I could wake up with a clear mind.

I told myself I was not going to drink coffee today, but when I got up, I had decided that I was going to drink a ton of the stuff. I needed to figure this all out today. I still hadn't decided whether I was going to help myself. We pulled up in front of the house, I reached over and kissed her good bye and ran into the house. I went straight for the bedroom, and fell into my bed. I rolled around for a while then the darkness enveloped me. I had a few dreams that I cannot recall, but I had the feeling they were distorted. I know that dreaming is a way for the brain to release memories.

I opened my eyes and looked at the clock. 9:19 PM was the time. I noticed there was a bottle of pills next to my clock on the nightstand. I reached over and grabbed the bottle and read the instructions. It was dark in the room, but my eyes could focus on the 'take three times daily after meals' on the label. I didn't eat three times a day. I usually only ate breakfast and dinner. But doctor's orders right, so I decided I was going to start eating lunch.

I sat up and rubbed my eyes. I wandered into the kitchen, and looked over the half wall that separated the living room from the kitchen. Anna had fallen asleep on the couch watching television. I was going to make some coffee, but then thought better of it.

I wandered over to the sink and filled up a glass of water. I opened my new found hope in a pill bottle, and down the recommended dose. I put the pills down next to the sink. I tiptoed over to the living room. I pulled the blanket from the top of the couch and laid it over my sleeping wife's body. I then grabbed the remote and sat down in my recliner.

I flipped through the channels for a while. I didn't even bother checking any of the financial channels. I was beginning to care less and less about the market. I knew my money was safe, and it was going to continue with a good return whether or not I watched the markets. I stopped channel surfing when I came upon a channel that was running a Three Stooges marathon. I love the three stooges, Moe, Larry, and Curly, of course, not Shemp or Cousin Joe. I watched the marathon for a few hours.

I got to thinking about the pill I had taken. If it worked, then I would not have to worry about my reflection's request tomorrow morning. I began to think about why he wanted to meet me in the first place. He had said he wanted to find someone. Who could he possibly find on this side that is not on his side? The story he told me about how things were was sort of confusing too. I mean, if I had everything going for me over here, and he got the short end of the stick, that meant that I had all the control. So, it wasn't exactly a different world. It seems the world over there is just a mixed-up effect of my side, which means that side is the reaction from my action. Newton's laws, every action has an equal and opposite reaction. That was holding true from my reflection's point of view.

I sat there and thought about the whole situation for a long time. Finally, I decided I would get up, eat breakfast, take a pill, and then meet my reflection at 8 AM. If nothing happened, then I would know that I am going crazy. It would also mean that the pills are working. If something did happen, then I would fulfill *my* request to switch sides. He told me he wouldn't bother me ever again, as long I helped him out. He stole from me already, so how much more damage could he do?

Whatever happened would be worth it if I never had to deal with this again. It was fun and exciting to explore a new world, but it was becoming harder to focus between reality and fiction. I could see my wife was becoming more and more stressed out, and I couldn't talk to anyone about anything that was happening.

The doctor was a good idea. If the pills worked then it would be worth every penny for my insurance carrier. If the pills didn't work it would still be worth the money because I was able to tell someone whom I didn't know about my experiences. The key part of telling someone I didn't know; was that I didn't have to see that person day in and day out. Not to mention; the doctor/client privilege which protected my rights. I knew that he wouldn't tell anyone. The funniest thing about all this; is today I want to tell everyone what has happened. You can call me crazy, but I call it; just warning people about the things in life that are unexplainable.

I reached over and woke up Anna. I told her she should come to bed. She stumbled past me into the bathroom to brush her teeth. I let her finish and then I went in after her. I went to the sink to brush my teeth, and started staring at myself. I began to think to myself that I would be there at 8 AM next day like we agreed. I didn't hear any other thoughts come back into my head, so I started thinking that maybe the pill was working. I finished brushing my teeth, and was about to leave the bathroom, but I stopped and looked at myself one more time. I pointed to myself and said, "I got your number!"

I turned off the light and headed for my bedroom. I kissed my wife good night even though she was almost asleep again. I rolled over and looked at my clock; it read 2:47 AM. I was about to close my eyes and then remembered I had better set the alarm. I reached over and fumbled with the buttons for a few minutes. It had been so long since I set the thing, that I almost forgot how to do it. I was satisfied with 7 AM, this way I would have enough time to make some breakfast, take my pill, and drink some coffee. I was pretty proud of myself; I had not had one cup of coffee all day. I was breaking almost every part of my daily routine lately. I felt good, my head hurt a little, but I know it was just a caffeine headache. It was nothing an Advil or Tylenol couldn't fix.

I put my head into my pillow, and thought about how the next day would turn out. Luckily, I had taken a nap earlier; otherwise, the next day would not have seemed so interesting. I needed to get a few more hours of sleep before the sun rose again. No matter what the results were going to be, I needed to be well rested. Ready for anything, was the last thing I thought about before my eyes closed for the night.

CHAPTER 6

The beeping from the alarm echoed in the distance. I could hear it in my dream, like it was the background sound in a thunderstorm. I opened my eyes slowly. My eyelids felt really heavy. I reached over and slammed my hand down on the snooze button. I closed my eyes and dozed off for a few minutes; I sat up really quick thinking I had fallen asleep longer than I actually did. Have you ever fallen back asleep after the alarm goes off in the morning? The weird thing is that you could have a whole dream in the amount of time it takes for your clock's snooze button to go off again.

I yawned and rubbed my burning eyes. I knew I needed to sleep a little longer for my health's sake, but I also knew that today was going to be the first day of my new life. I got up and wandered into the kitchen to take my medication. I ran some water from the faucet until it felt cold to the touch. Then I swallowed my pill and just hoped it was going to work. I almost didn't care about my reflection's request for a meeting. I wanted to go back to bed. Even though I took that nap yesterday, I had that sleepy feel in my sights.

I was going to meet myself in the bathroom as planned, but I hoped that the medication would stop another experience. If it did, then I would be able to say I was just going crazy. Truthfully, it was beginning to sound like a good idea. I would not have minded telling this story if I knew I was crazy. Then it could be one of those humorous stories that people talk about some night out on the town when they drank too much.

I fixed myself some eggs and bacon. I burnt the toast, and didn't feel like making anymore. I sat at my kitchen table eating my eggs and bacon. I didn't make any coffee; I hadn't had any in two days and this was the third. I was beginning to feel really good inside. The water actually tasted good without any color. I finished my breakfast and put my dishes in the dishwasher.

I was standing over the sink wondering about my life and realizing how screwed up it had become in the past four days. I decided to go into the bathroom and then I talked myself out of that idea as quickly as I had talked myself into it. Then I wanted to go out of curiosity, just to see if the medication was working properly.

The battle in my mind waged on for a long time. Finally, I had a moment of clarity. I realized I had to face myself sooner or later. I mean, what else could I do? Was I going to spend the rest of my life running from myself? He wasn't in control; I had all the power, he even said that in the conversation we had in my head. That makes me sound crazy, doesn't it?

Well, I pushed my fears and anger down into my gut. I pushed off the kitchen sink and glanced at the clock on the stove. 7:58 AM. It was time to straighten out the whole ordeal. I cautiously walked towards the bathroom not knowing what to expect.

I peeked around the corner like a little kid playing war. I don't know what I was looking for, but the coast was clear. I straightened up and then entered the bathroom like everything was normal. Even though in the back of my mind I knew it was not.

I walked over to the sink and looked at myself in the mirror. I remember thinking or hoping my new medication was going to work. I smiled at myself, and then I grabbed my toothbrush and started to do my normal bathroom routine.

When I finished rinsing my mouth out, I reached over and grabbed the hand towel off the rack to wipe off the water that was left behind on my chin. I smiled at myself, and then gave myself the thumbs up.

"Well, I am here like you asked. What's the plan?"

I waited and waited for a few minutes and then I let out a sigh of relief. Nothing had happened, and I didn't mind either. I bowed my head and laughed at myself. It was beginning to look like the medication was my solution all along.

I must have blinked because in an instant I was looking at a second pair of feet, except they were not my wife's feet or my own for that matter. That would have been a sight for sore eyes. I followed my sight up the legs and then my worst fear was standing in front of me. There he was the downfall of my perfect existence. I realized the medication was not working, and I didn't know what to say or do. Someone had popped my balloon full of hopes and dreams.

Well, I was not crazy; that is what I learned at that very moment in my life. The medication was taken as prescribed, and yet here I was standing on the other side of my mirror. The medication was not a solution. It was just a waste of time and money that I can never get back. This is what I feared most, because it meant that I was on my own. There would not be quick fix to my problem. Either I was going to fix it or I was going to die trying. I figured there would not be a point in living out this type of existence day in and day out. Then the first moment of what I have termed, "My New Life" happened.

I didn't hesitate, and in a split second I punched my reflection as hard as I could. I watched him fly across the bathroom and into the wall.

Immediately I felt the heat in my own face where my fist hit his. I reached up and touched my face and felt the swelling. I looked over and my reflection was doing the same thing. He let out a laugh, which only angered me more. I charged over to him and started punching him repeatedly in the face. The whole time I was beating him up; I could feel the pain in my own face. Finally, I stopped and let go of his shirt. I stepped back and fell to the floor.

"Do you feel better now?" He asked.

"NO!" I screamed back.

"Well, I guess I deserve it. I have not been too straight with you about all of this." He spoke.

"That's the understatement of the year. I thought I was crazy! Don't get me wrong, this would be great for someone like Stephen King, but this is not something that happens to sane people." I spoke.

"Well, actually; it could, but I found a way to access your side. If others from over here could figure that out, I am sure they would do the same as me." He spoke.

"Yeah, and then, there would be total chaos. We are not the same people. We are two different people who have a few coincidences. I mean, you are a fuck up, and I am the brains of this operation." I yelled.

"The brains; that remains to be seen. You can't control our little rendezvous, so tell me who is smarter?" He chirped out with heavy sarcasm.

"I know I can fall asleep right now, and back I go. I know that much." I said trying to sound like I knew what I was talking about.

"Good, at least you have been paying attention. How do you think I pull you through the mirror?" He asked.

"I haven't figured that part out yet." I said quietly.

"Ha, the brains, huh? Well, truth is, you want to be pulled through the mirror. Otherwise, I would have no power to do it. You see this is mutual; your life is boring and uneventful. You have been looking for an escape. I have given you the ultimate vacation, and yet you are so ungrateful. You are like that kid who gets everything he asks for, but truthfully he is still unhappy because he doesn't have everything." He yelled back.

"Vacation, grateful? You are so fucked up! You call all the crap you have done to me in the past four days a vacation? What do I have to be thankful to you for? Hold on, let me guess, oh yeah how about sleeping with my wife for starters? No, no, how about when you are stealing my money? Or what about making me look crazy to everyone I know? Yeah, I am so sorry, you are my savior. Fuck You!" I screamed as I stood up.

"What are you going to do, beat us up again? Your face looks like mine. Now I am going to have to make up some spectacular story just so Anna doesn't admit us into a psych ward." He said as he motioned for me to sit back down.

"You are not telling Anna a damn thing. You stay away from my wife. You fucking hear me?" I screamed as I pointed at him.

"Look man, that was fun for the first night or so, but that is not why I need your help. Keep your wife; I was married to her once too." He whispered as he looked down in his lap.

"How's that, I saw her at the strip club when we left the hospital." I spoke.

His head bounced up really fast at the sound of that. I could tell I had struck a nerve in him. I had never seen him react normally to something I said or did. But when I spoke of Anna on this side, I could see the same emotion I had about my Anna on the other side.

"Is that where you were? What strip club were you at? I need to know, now!" He said adamantly.

"I ain't tellin' you shit; until I get some answers of my own; got it, so we are going to play a little game called show and tell. I ask something, you answer it, and then so on and so forth. Got it!" I sneered.

"Alright, I got some time, fire away." He spoke.

"First, why did you really need my help? I know it is not to find someone on my side. What's the real reason?" I asked.

"That is the real reason. I need to find this guy Dagger." He answered.

"Why?" I asked.

"So, I can kill him." He calmly said with disdain in his eyes.

I was stunned by the answer. It was the furthest thing from my mind. I sat back down and tried to figure out where this was going. It was not turning out the way I had planned, but at least I was working with myself and not against.

"If you kill someone on my side, and then come back, then I am left with the mess. They would really think I was crazy if I told them that you killed the guy, and I had no recollection of it." I said.

"That was my plan. I mean we would be sent to a psych ward because nobody would believe you. They would think you had lost your mind. So, we sit in the mental institute for a few years, and I leave you alone. Then slowly you would have started to show signs of improvement. We would be released and back to business as usual, except, Dagger would be dead on your side, and also on mine." He replied.

"Who is this guy Dagger? Why would you want him dead? I mean every time you answer one of my questions; I end up with ten new ones. Wait, do I even want to know why you want him dead?" I asked.

"Probably not." He said.

"Okay, well how could we fix this problem without killing this guy?" I felt like I was starting to make some progress with my interrogation of myself. Sooner or later, he was going to have to fill me in on everything. I was losing patience with the whole situation.

"I owe him 500 stacks." He said in a disappointed tone.

"Well, is that all?" I said, as I slapped my hands on my knees. "You stole at least 5000 from me already. 500 bucks should be no problem." I laughed.

He raised his eyebrows and I could see his eyes. They made me feel like he was looking through me instead of at me. Then he stood up, and walked over to me. He put his hand on my shoulder as he kneeled down to eye level again.

"500 stacks is five hundred thousand dollars." He said in the calmest manner I had ever seen him.

"What?" I had nothing else to say. Five hundred thousand dollars; the number went through my head over and over again. I couldn't even fathom how someone could have accumulated that kind of a debt.

"So, you were going to kill this guy? Was it over drugs?" I asked with a little calmer attitude.

"Yep, lots and lots of heroin. I spent all the money we made in our little business venture, and then I lost the house, the furniture, the cars, and finally the wife to that sorry son of a bitch. I am going to gut that fat fuck on your side, because then I know he will die on this side. You understand me now!" He said with such a conviction, I was almost speechless.

Then I felt his hand leave my shoulder as he stood up. I had the feeling like something bad was going to happen, but when I opened my mouth to say something; he disappeared to other side of the mirror. I jumped up and looked at him through the mirror. I was so pissed at that moment. I had let him get away. If he went and killed this guy he was talking about, I would be in a whole new world of problems. I had to stop him somehow. I was afraid to leave the bathroom. I started thinking about how much trouble it might be to let him leave. I knew as long as I stood in front of that mirror, he was not going to be able to go anywhere.

There I stood for a long time staring at myself while I questioned everything that was said. I wondered what I could possibly do to stop him from killing this guy on my side. First, I figured maybe I could find him first, and as long as I avoided all mirrors along the way I might be able to figure it out. This way when I did find him, I would go in front of a mirror and my reflection would have to do what I did.

I mean I had control, so if I wanted to keep him alive, I would be able too. There were too many possible outcomes I couldn't control with this solution, so I continued to think. How do I find a guy who sells drugs? I mean I can't just walk up and down the blocks of Chicago asking everyone I see if they know a guy named Dagger who sells heroin. Also, I asked myself why my reflection didn't kill this guy on his side. Obviously, he was in contact with him over here...

"Look, he is way too powerful on that side." My reflection chimed in my head. "I would have done it by now, but I am hoping he is not in the same business over here. This way he won't be packing any heat or have a ton of guys around him at all times. Now quit thinking about how to stop me, you may have control, but I have the power to read your mind while we stand looking at each other. You might be able to control the actions in front of mirrors, but I can control a hell of a lot more. As you have seen."

"Okay smart ass! We can figure something else out. I don't think killing this guy is the right way to go. Maybe we can pay him?" I said. The thought just slipped from my lips without a moment's hesitation. It is like my mouth was working for my brain.

"I don't have that kind of money, Charlie, maybe you do, but I don't." He said in reply to my vocalized comment.

"Well, that's just it, I do. All right since you are over there, and to show you good faith on my part, go find my broker's phone number on the fridge. Call him up and tell him you want to make a withdrawal from the account. And just so you don't have a grand plan of taking more than you should, I know it cannot happen today. Maybe tomorrow at the earliest, I mean, you know that financial institutions do not like to give away large amounts of money. It will have to be approved and then it goes through. So, you make the call, so you see I am not bullshitting you. This way you don't have to get me in all kinds of trouble. Personally, I don't want to spend my retirement in a psych ward. What do you think?" I asked.

"It might work, as long as you're on the level." He replied, "You are in my head. You would know if I wasn't." I said sarcastically.

"Alright, but you got to stay in the room today. No matter what, Dagger has been looking for me. When you said that Anna was working in a strip club, it all made sense." He said.

"What made sense?" I asked not knowing what I was going to hear.

"Dagger is her pimp. She is working that club for tricks, which means if she saw you then she probably said something to him. She is fucked up; I mean she has got to be strung out bad. It is my fault but I can't do anything to save her until I save myself." He said.

I was still stuck on the word "pimp," and I missed everything else he said. I have to tell you though that my recollection of everything that was said between myself and I is exact. For some reason, I am able to recall all the conversations verbatim.

Well, I let him call my broker and I went into the motel room to chill out. I knew if I wanted to go back all I had to do was fall asleep, which was not going to be too hard since I was dead tired already from the rude awakening, I got from my alarm clock. I walked out of the bathroom thinking about what I had told him to do. I had the worst feeling in my stomach like I was making a serious mistake. I thought about falling asleep right away so I could stop everything. Then I figured I would give him the benefit of the doubt. I mean I could always change my mind if I felt like it. All I would have to do is call my broker tomorrow and tell him to cancel the transaction. That thought made me feel a little better about my choice.

I sat on the edge of the bed in silence while my brain concocted idea after idea. More and more questions went through my head. This whole ordeal was killing me a lot faster than my retirement. Yeah, I found out that police officers have the highest quickest death rate after retiring than any other profession. I know this has nothing to do with my story but I thought it was interesting when I read that.

I guess a lot of cops commit suicide and they cannot handle retiring from their profession. It becomes a second lifestyle for most, which says a lot about cops. I have to give them a lot of credit for the job they do, even though I did run into some real assholes while I dealt with myself during that week of Christmas in '99.

So, I finally got bored of thinking about all the bad things, and I needed something to take my mind off of the situation. I looked up at the television, and found my savior. I was sure there was not cable but it didn't matter. The news would be fine. I could always get the Dow Jones Industrial Average numbers from the news. I clicked on the television, and I was surprised there were a few channels that were cable. There was just a couple of movie channels and CNN. I stopped on CNN and watched the broadcast.

"Today, the White House press secretary told reporters that President Miller would be traveling to Chicago this weekend to speak with Mayor Martinez about the new federal education bill that Democrats are trying to push through Congress. President Miller will be discussing the pitfalls of privatizing the public schools across the nation."

"President Miller?" I said out loud to myself.

I was blown away; I guess this world was far different from mine. I watched the news with an added interest. I felt like I did when I was kid learning how to swing a bat for little league for the first time. It was exciting to be somewhere else; especially since I knew nothing about this place, I had visited a few times already. The names that went across the screen and the stories the reporter told were so funny. I didn't understand how different everything was until I watched story after story.

I continued to watch the news for a good hour or so. Which probably was not the greatest idea of mine, but then I had a real thought. I was so curious about how different everything actually was, that I got the urge to get my hands on a history book. I started thinking about how I could go about reading about this world. I figured I would start with the daily newspaper. I figured that would be a great read. I know I was supposed to stay inside but going out for a newspaper and maybe even a cup of coffee was sounding like a great idea to me.

I turned off the television, and grabbed a jacket. I opened the door, and then I shut it after realizing I didn't have the motel room key. I ran around the room with such haste; I felt like I was on an Easter egg hunt. I couldn't find the key, so I just left the door unlocked and wandered around the neighborhood looking for a coffee shop or corner store. I went down Elston the last time, and there was nothing down that way that I could remember seeing, so I headed north up Milwaukee Avenue. I passed the McDonald's, even though they had coffee, I remembered a Dunkin Donuts on Nagle and Devon by Superdawg, and I figured the stores had almost been the same so I probably had a pretty good shot at getting some D & D coffee.

I trudged up Milwaukee Avenue, and watched the cars drive by me. It was cold out but it didn't bother me because there was no wind blowing. I walked for what seemed like twenty minutes or so. Then I spotted the Burger King which I was familiar with, and right next door in the next lot was Dunkin Donuts. What a relief that was to see with my eyes. I was starting to get cold by the time I came up on Nagle Avenue.

I crossed Milwaukee Avenue and entered Dunkin Donuts and ordered a large regular with cream and extra sugar. I got my change and coffee and wandered outside to the paper machine. I bought a Sun-Times newspaper; luckily the paper names were the same; then I went back inside and sat down to drink my coffee and read the paper. I didn't mind wasting time here now that I was becoming accustomed to my second world.

I flipped through the paper and read everything including the advertisements. I was really interested in how different some things were, yet a lot of stuff was still the same. I tried to think about how different everything actually was here and also how it all came to be this way. I mean, I remember in the beginning of that week when my reflection told me about how I had made all the right choices in life, and thus forced him to make the wrong choices. If this was the case for me, then I started imagining how that might be true for everyone else.

Israel had allowed Palestine to declare statehood, which caused many other Arab countries to befriend Israel. This blew my mind but the weirdest story I read about was a historical archive that had been reprinted. It was a story about the Great Chicago Fire. The article was a reprint from some newspaper that was found in the vaults of the Sun-Times. It told the story a little different that I had known it. I guess there was a bar-fight on the South Side of Chicago, and it spilled out into the street. The loser from that fight got angry and lit the bar on fire. This sparked off the neighboring buildings, and the wind was blowing from the South that night which carried the flames. I had never heard about anything like that, which made me dream of how long the other side of the mirror had existed.

I finished reading the paper and polished off the coffee. I got up to leave and grabbed one more coffee for the cold walk back to the motel. I figured I had more than enough time to take a shower and at the same time I could get an update from me on the other side. This way I would be able to know what the next move would be. I knew the money would not be available for withdrawal until tomorrow at the earliest.

I grabbed my coffee and started walking down Milwaukee Avenue again. I took my time getting back to the Esquire Motel. I looked around with a renewed interest in my surroundings. I made it back without doing any serious damage to myself, which had been the theme up until today. I hit the bend in the sidewalk where Elston Avenue breaks off Milwaukee Avenue. I could see the motel as I approached it. I had hoped the cleaning lady had not come by the room. If she locked the door then I would have to go to the office, and as much as I was beginning to feel comfortable in my new world, I still didn't want to have to deal with too many people who already dealt with my reflection on a regular basis. We may look alike but are personalities are definitely two different people.

I crossed the side street and walked towards my room. There was a brand-new Cadillac SUV parked in front of my room. It wasn't there when I left, but I just looked at it and didn't even put two and two together. I reached for the door handle on my door and opened the door.

Two hands grabbed me and then tossed me across the room into kitchen counter. I heard the door slam, and my eyes slowly focused on the two big individuals standing over me. I looked up just in time to see a steel-toed boot get pressed into the side of my head. I was being held to the carpet by a pair size 13 boots. The only reason I know the size is because I could read the bottom of the sole since it was right on top of my eye. I could no longer see who the two guys were; my only line of sight was the door, carpeting, and the very large sole of a boot across my face.

The one holding me down didn't say anything the whole time. The other guy, who I had only glanced at before I was staring at rubber, started asking me questions about his money. I immediately knew exactly whom I was dealing with. I called him out by his name, Dagger; I didn't want to make him suspicious since we had never actually met before.

He asked me about his money and told me my time was up. I tried to tell him that it was in the works, and he went on and on about how I had told him that for the past two months. Since I disappeared two weeks ago, there was no point in believing anything I said any longer. I was out of options. I couldn't tell him who I really was, because that probably would have gotten me killed that day. So, I stayed quiet for the most part. Except when I was getting kicked in the stomach, which is when I couldn't help but let out a few yelps in pain.

I kept pleading for him to believe that he would have his money within the next twenty-four hours. I said I was working on getting him his five hundred thousand, and then we would be even. I guess it worked because the boot was removed from my face after I said that.

I sat up and put my back up against the cabinet. I figured I would stay on the floor, since I didn't want this guy to feel threatened. I mean I was scared, probably the most scared I had ever been in my entire life. I focused on him as he went towards the window to sit down in one of the chairs by the table. I rubbed my face and gave the other guy standing over me a dirty look. As much as I was scared, I still wanted to give back the same treatment. I understood why my reflection wanted to kill this guy.

I looked back at Dagger. Now Dagger was a black guy. Dagger stood six foot three inches tall. His hair was faded and he as big as an inmate being released from a ten-year bit. He was wearing all black. A black leather trench coat to be exact, it covered his entire frame, and enveloped his black t-shirt and black jeans. Even his boots were black. He was a scary guy to look at from my point of view. In all my years of existence I had never run across someone like him.

He sat down and it was kind of hard to focus on his face since the drapes were drawn and the light from outside was filtered through the thick fabric. I did my best though, and I really didn't want to see him anyway. He repeated the number five hundred thousand dollars a few times in a row. I was very confused since I could tell he was as sure about the number as I was. He started telling me that five hundred thousand would suffice but I had better have within 24 hours. He looked at his watch, and then looked at me, and then he told me he was even going to do me a favor. He was going to give me until noon tomorrow. If I didn't have the money in his hands by noon tomorrow, then there would be nowhere I could go that he wouldn't search for me.

I believed him, and then I started praying that my reflection was doing what we decided he should do. If a phone call had not been made to my broker in time, there would not be enough time to make the withdrawal. I needed to talk to myself as soon as possible, which meant I was going to have to get these two thugs out of my way. I tried to push them out the door with my words, but Dagger wasn't budging. He called out his buddy's name, Visshes; and then looked at me.

He told me, I had made the smartest move I could have, that is offering him double the money in order to get an extra 24 hours of life. That really confused me for a few seconds, and then I realized that I had duped me yet again. I reiterated that I only owed two hundred and fifty thousand just to make sure. Dagger nodded in approval, and then he told me it was five hundred now. I nodded in approval, hoping to get rid of these guys as soon as possible. I asked if they would come and pick it up tomorrow, and Dagger let out a huge laugh as he told his buddy how much a jokester I was. Dagger looked at me and then told me I had to deliver it.

He also said that I should consider it a tax for being such a junkie scumbag. I took offense to that because he had no idea who he was dealing with, but I took it as my way out. I agreed and laughed. I remember telling him I needed to get going so I could get his money without any problems. I didn't want to tell him where the money was coming from, and I am glad he didn't ask me. I didn't know what I would have told him. I was still confused, and my ribs and face hurt. Dagger stood up, buttoned up his jacket and headed for the door. I looked at Visshes to follow him, but he just stood there giving me a really hard look. Dagger told me as he opened the door that I had better be on time tomorrow or I would not be in good standing with him anymore. I let out a laugh because I figured I already wasn't in good standing. Dagger turned to look at me with a sharp glance. I looked into his eyes and chills went down my spine. He pointed at me as if to say, "Watch it."

I stopped laughing and then went to stand up. Visshes took a step towards me and pulled a pistol from his waistband. I looked at Dagger who was already climbing into the Black SUV outside, and then back at Visshes. The handle of that silver plated gun hit me square in the temple. Now I thought a hit to the temple could kill a man, but I found out that day, it really just hurts a lot and leaves one hell of a bruise. I fell back to the floor and grabbed my head. I could feel the blood dribbling down my face, and the pain was excruciating. I watched Visshes stroll out of the room and then he slammed the door behind him. I could hear the truck start up and then they peeled out.

I sat on the floor for a long time. I took my hand from the side of my face and looked at the blood that covered my hand. I was pissed. Yet there was nothing I could do. I knew I would have to fall asleep in order to get back to my side. I also wanted to tell myself off, especially for lying to me about the amount of money owed to that son of a bitch, Dagger. I wanted to get up and go to the bathroom, but I didn't feel good. My head was pounding. I felt like I had been given a pile driver. It felt like my world had been spun upside down and slammed on top of my head. I had a headache that proved that.

I stood up and used the countertop for support while I fumbled through the drawers looking for a paper towels, rags, or napkins. Pretty much anything I could use to put on my head. I found a rag and turned on the faucet. I put my head underneath the running water and it was cold. It felt really good. I washed off the blood and then held the rag under the water to get it wet. I put it up against my latest war wound. I opened up the mini-fridge and checked the icebox for some ice. I was not surprised to find that there was no ice in the box, but there was a bottle of whiskey and two bottles of beer in the fridge. I grabbed the whiskey and put it up against my head. I stood there for a second thinking about grabbing a beer, but I was never much of a drinker. I finally reached down with my other hand and grabbed a bottle of beer. I stood up, kicked the door closed and stumbled over to the bed to sat down. I wanted to go into the bathroom, but like I said a few minutes ago, I was pissed and didn't even want to look at myself right then and there.

I had a brainstorm of an idea and went outside. I stood at my door, and glanced around the parking lot. There were no cars in the lot, only on Elston waiting for the light to turn green. I looked at the lead car and the passenger was an old lady who looked at me funny. Here I was with a bloody rag held to the side of my face. I was sure my face was beginning to swell. I took the rag off of my face, and then yelled at her to go and quit looking at me. That is the moment that I realized I was changing. I was becoming my reflection, and I didn't like it. The car drove off, and I must have scared her because she quit looking at me.

I wandered over to one of the snow banks that were obviously built by some snowplow during the last snowfall. I reached down and grabbed a hand full of snow. I began to pack it into a flat snowball. I put the rag in my pocket and started to hold the snow to my head. It felt really good. I stood there for a minute and then looked up and was about to say something to God, but stopped when I saw the billboard attached to the neighboring building.

There in huge letters right above me was a crime stoppers sign. It had a phone number on it that you could call if you knew of any illegal activity. The smaller letters on the board told me I could stay anonymous if I didn't want to divulge who I was. Trust me when I tell you, that should have been a sign on what to do next, but it wasn't. Hindsight is 20/20; remember when I said that earlier. Well, it is the truth. I wandered back into the room and slammed the door so hard the walls shook.

I threw the rag on the table and tossed the melting snowball into the sink. I realized it was time for me to face myself. I needed answers and I wanted them now. I walked into the bathroom and looked at myself. I laughed because I had forgotten that he looked liked me. I totally forgot about being mad for a second while I thought about how he might have gotten the knot on his head. Of course, the knot I am referring to; was different form the knots I gave myself earlier. I looked at the mirror and then recalled my little trip to Dunkin Donuts. I remembered how the cashier had looked at me funny, and I didn't put it together until now. I looked like shit, but the funny thing is, I felt worse inside than I did outside. Every day was becoming one painful experience after another.

"So why didn't you tell me it was only 250 STACKS!" I emphasized the word I didn't understand earlier.

"What happened? How did you find out about that?" He asked me, which really pissed me off.

"Your buddy just paid me a visit. We had a nice little talk, and then I got this." I turned my head, so I could see the huge gash in my temple.

"Yeah, I slipped on some ice in the driveway." He replied to me, laughing while he spoke.

I couldn't help but laugh in disbelief, because this ordeal was obviously causing him pain also. I bowed my head and tried to clear my mind hoping the pain would go away. I sat there for a few minutes without saying a word, and then I picked up my head and was thankful he didn't break the silence. I looked into my eyes and then realized we were still in this together. No matter how pissed I could get, it wouldn't make any difference concerning the problem at hand.

"Alright, Dagger came by, I didn't have all the information, and so I told him we would pay him five hundred thousand by tomorrow. We have until noon to get it to him." I said.

"You told him that. Are you stupid?" He started yelling, but he could tell I was about to blow. "Look, I am sorry for not leveling with you, I figured since you were offering, I could set a little aside for myself. You can relate to that, can't you?"

He could tell by my face that I could not relate to his idiotic thinking patterns. He knew I was the calm collected one, which is why I was not in his situation. I mean if I had not been so calm and collected the roles might have been reversed. But they were not and I said it earlier, I knew I was the brain of the operation. If things were going to work out for both of us then I had better start making them work out as best as I could.

"Did you call my broker?" I asked.

"Yeah, he wants me to come in tomorrow morning at 9 AM to sign all the papers. Then he is going to write out the check. Since I knew, the bank would not want to cash something that big, I told him to phone ahead and clear it up today. He asked me what I needed all the money for. I told him it was none of his fucking business and to just do his job." He finished with a serious look.

"You didn't say that did you?" I asked.

"Naw, I am just messing with you. I told him I was making a move into some new business venture. Then he asked me why I couldn't just transfer the money electronically, and then I responded with a little well-known trick I learned in drug dealing. I told him to not ask about information he really doesn't want to know about." He said to me.

"Well, that is not much better; it sounds like we are up to no good." I replied with a little fear in my voice.

"Yeah, well we are." He replied.

"I need to come back; I am going to try and go to sleep, alright. I will do the transfer in the morning. We can meet tomorrow as soon as it is done. I will use the bank restroom, and then we can figure the

rest out. I am sure you know this, but the head is hurting really bad."
I said as I pointed to my head.

"Look there is some Vicodin in nightstand by the bed. Take two
of them bad boys and you will be dreaming in about 45 minutes."
He was about to say something else but was cut off by Anna yelling
through the door.

She was asking who he was talking to, and that is when I realized
how much I missed my wife. I wanted my life back. I wanted to quit
leaving my world to come over into this one. I was getting very tired
of getting hurt all the time. Boredom was one thing, but at least I
knew how to deal with that. Sooner or later all these head injuries
were going to add up to some serious brain damage or death. The
latter was not an option.

I put my two fingers up to my temple and gave a good-bye salute.
I staggered out of the bathroom back into a solo existence. I checked
the drawer of the nightstand and I did find the bottle of Vicodin just
like he said. I took out two pills and ran some water in the sink. I
cupped a handful of water and downed the pills. I was never good
at taking pills. They always seemed to get lodged at the back of my
throat. I would gag a lot when I was kid and I had to take aspirin.
These pills were huge, Vicodin are like horse pills. But I had no
trouble swallowing them; I guess I just had too many other things
going through my mind.

I walked back to the bed and thought about the whole turn of
events. I was about to take a third of my retirement money out of my
account and give it away. The interest alone on five hundred thousand
dollars brings in every year is about thirty thousand dollars. I knew
giving the money away was going to create more problems with Anna
than I cared to think about. I could feel the pills starting to take effect,
so I rolled onto my back and looked at the ceiling.

I waited for my eyelids to get heavy, and when that started to
happen, I tried to clear my mind of all the garbage that was flowing

through it. I remember my last thoughts on that December 21st morning was of Anna. It was the first day of winter, and here I was caught in two different worlds with nowhere to go but down. I felt like I was on a roller coaster and I knew it was going to crash. I had to find that balance I had been searching for since the whole ordeal had begun. I felt my eyes close and then oblivion came and let me tell you, it was not soon enough.

CHAPTER 7

I awoke from a heavy sleep. My eyelids didn't open right away, but I was awake. My first thoughts that morning revolved around my pounding head. The pain was everywhere, and I didn't want to move. I slowly opened my eyes and couldn't focus on anything right away. The light from outside was really bright and caused me to squint immediately. The light made my head hurt even more. I felt like I was hung over. My mouth was really dry, and I felt dehydrated. I turned my head to look at the clock. 9:30 AM.

The sight of the clock's time made me jump up with such haste. I felt a lot of blood rush to my head, and the effects of moving quickly did not help my cause. I sat there and dropped my head while I massaged the back of my neck. My head hurt badly, along with all the bruises I could feel throbbing on my face. I swung my feet over the side of the bed and sat there trying to focus and find some motivation to move. I knew I had to get that money. I was not sure if my reflection gets killed, does that mean I die too. I assumed that was the case, and I was going to make sure I didn't find out the hard way.

I stood up slowly, and used the bed for support. I stumbled into the kitchen. I wanted to call out for Anna, but my throat was hoarse and my cottonmouth made it tough to speak. I walked over the sink and turned on the faucet. I ran the water for a few seconds for it to get cold. I cupped some water and drank a mouthful. The water slid down my throat with such a soothing feeling. I immediately felt better. I went to the cupboard for a glass, and then I noticed a note from Anna on the countertop.

> *Dear Jack,*
>
> *I had to run some errands. You have been really distant lately and we need to talk about some things that are going on. Please take your medication. I will be home in a few hours; I plan on sitting down and discussing our lives today. You haven't spoken to me very much lately, and I love you and want to know where you are at, in your head.*
>
> *Love,*
> *Anna*

The funny thing about that letter was she wanted to know what was going on in my head. At the time, I didn't know what was going on in my head. I wanted to let her know about everything, but it was becoming a constant battle for me to just stay in tune. I was getting better and I knew that I needed to get that money. I wish I could have stayed and waited for Anna to get back that day, but I knew it was either life or death for me to finish what I started yesterday.

I took my medication; I mean it didn't work the day before, but I wanted to not have to lie to Anna later. Hell, it wasn't even a solution. It was really just one more problem to add to the long list already forming with every minute that passed. I pulled myself together, my headache was fading to the back of my brain, and my eyes didn't hurt as bad. I grabbed the cordless phone and dialed my broker's number.

It turned out that my reflection did a really great job impersonating me. My broker had made the arrangements with LaSalle Bank's downtown branch to give me the funds in cash. The conversation on the phone lasted a little longer than I had anticipated, but I couldn't just leave him hanging. I was withdrawing a lot of money from my retirement fund, and I didn't like it one bit. I knew that when I had to tell Anna, it was going to be the hardest thing I would ever have to do.

I hardly ever drove, but since Anna was not around, I was going to have to drive myself downtown. I didn't have very much time to waste, so I hurried back into my bedroom grabbed a hooded sweatshirt and ran into the bathroom to brush my teeth. I stood there in front of the mirror and began to brush my teeth. I looked into my eyes and could see the stress in both of us. The bags around my eyes were swollen and black. I obviously was not sleeping well anymore. Not to mention, I looked like I had taken on the Chicago Blackhawks in a fistfight.

With the toothbrush in my hand, I reached down to cup some water in my hand. I filled up mouth and then swished it around in my mouth. I bent my head down and spit out the water in the sink. I placed my toothbrush back into the holder and looked at myself one last time before I left to give away a half a million dollars to myself.

I blinked and then realized my reflection had jumped the gun. I looked out the door and saw the motel room. I looked back at him as he shrugged his shoulders. I remember screaming the word, "NO." How could he double cross me? After everything I was going to do for him, I was about to lose my mind.

"Sorry, I have to do this. I didn't think you would." He said to me.

"Didn't think I would? Are you kidding me? If you die, then I die. Why would I let that happen? I cannot believe you would double cross me like this. Well actually I can believe it, you are a piece of shit." I screamed.

"We are the same person, is that how you feel about yourself?" He said. I could hear him laughing in my head.

"I would have gotten the job done! You know what, I am sick of this shit. I am going to take some of those Vicodin. That will slow you down. Then we will see which one of us loses. You are such an impatient fool." I said finally satisfied with abusing myself.

"Just chill out in the room, and I will be back to meet you here in an hour or so." He said in a not so polite tone.

I was getting the feeling like he was treating me like a child. I was him, and yet, we were two totally different people. I realized that day just how vulnerable I was to the big picture. I was shelled and protected my entire life. My parents made sure I did the right things. I didn't just come out of the womb and decide I was never going to do anything wrong. Hell, I was capable of screwing up.

I got kicked out of kindergarten for punching a girl in the mouth. We had been standing in line waiting to file into the school one spring morning, and it was show-and-tell day. I had brought my favorite stuffed animal to school to show everyone who was my best friend. It was a three-foot high stuffed bunny. He had long legs and extra-long arms. Like I said, it was my favorite.

This girl behind me in line peeked into the bag because it was slung over my shoulder. Sort of like the way bums used to carry their sacks on a stick, slung over the shoulder so it doesn't slow you down. I turned around after I felt the tug on the bag. I didn't even hesitate; I just punched her in mouth. My mother was working that day, so the school called my grandmother. When she got there, they had me sitting in the principal's office.

After a very long conversation behind closed doors, my grandmother emerged from the principal's office and asked me why I did such a thing. I told her that my Uncle Jon had told me to never take shit from nobody. He didn't specify genders. Anyway, the school felt my violent behavior was not what the administration needed at the school. So, my mother had me transferred to a private school. It was a Catholic school, and even though I am not Catholic, I have to say I was better off for it. I learned a lot about life and consequences.

The bottom line, which I used in my business attitude, was

you could hurt people physically and get into a lot of trouble. So, I learned to manipulate my way to the top. I did this in everything I accomplished throughout life. I don't think I hurt anyone in the process. At least I don't think I did. The whole point here is that my reflection was acting like a parent. I was very capable of being a man. Standing in front of that mirror made me realize that I despised myself deep down. But instead of working through it positively, I decided the next time I would get my hands on me; I was going to kill me. That sounds funny, doesn't it? Well, it was the truth. That is how I felt at that very moment.

I stormed out of the bathroom and went straight for the nightstand drawer where I had gotten the Vicodin yesterday. I opened the drawer and to my surprise he had taken the bottle. I ran around the room like a crazy person looking for those pills. I spent at least a half an hour looking for them. I never found them, and finally got so pissed that I just sat down on the bed and put my head in my hands. I was lost.

If my former business partner had seen me that day, he would not have recognized me. I had a broken arm, my fists were all cut up, and my face was beaten on every side. I couldn't remember the last time I held my wife. I had such a great life before that first switch. Since then, I felt like I was on a roller coaster going straight to Hell without any stops.

I finally was able to have some rational thoughts. It took a while, but they came. I looked at the clock to check the time. 10:18 AM. I had a little less than two hours until one of us was going to have to face Dagger. I got up and thought about going back into the bathroom, but then realized that if I did, then it might screw up what my reflection was in the process of doing. I tried to believe he was going to be able to withdraw the money and be back in time to make the switch. He was the only one who knew how to pull me through the mirror. I knew how to make it all stop for a night, but then I couldn't remember anything until I woke up. I don't think I even dreamt on the way back to my side.

If I could figure out how to switch back and forth then I would be able to fix things a heck of a lot better. I wandered around the room pacing back and forth for what seemed like hours. But every time I looked at the clock only a few minutes had passed. I turned on the television, but I couldn't concentrate on anything. I was getting impatient and that was never a quality of mine. I was usually calm, cool, and collected at all times. That was the main reason I was able to retire early. In the middle of that thought there was a knock at the door.

The knock made my stomach do somersaults. I got nervous and looked over my shoulder at the clock. 10:43 AM. The time made me feel better. I knew that I was supposed to meet Dagger at noon, which gave me at least another hour. I got up and silently went to the window. I put my back up against the wall and slid over to where the drapes started. I tried to peek out the window without moving the drapes. I got a glimpse of the parking lot, but I couldn't see any cars.

Another knock came followed by a woman's voice. It was the cleaning lady; here I was getting all worked up for nothing. I walked over to the door and opened it. There was a tiny little Italian woman asking me if I needed clean towels. I was so relieved, I told her sure, and took them. She wheeled her cart down the sidewalk and I slammed the door.

I tossed the towels on the bed and laughed at myself. I felt like I was in some spy movie. I was looking over my shoulder, feeling the adrenaline pump through my veins from all the fear. I couldn't help but laugh at myself. I had to be the biggest idiot known to man. I got the strangest feeling like this was turning out to be a product of my mind again. It would have been an awakening if the door hadn't swung open and knocked me to the floor. But that is what happened.

I tried to lift myself up and glance over my shoulder at the same time. It was useless though because there was a boot in the back of my neck as quickly as the door had hit me. I heard Visshes say stay down if I knew what was good for me. I tell you what; I don't think I knew what was good for me anymore. I still tried to move by squirming, but it just made the pain worse on the back of my neck. I was finally able to pull my face out of the carpet and turn it sideways so I could see a little bit.

I saw Dagger's legs come into my view. I knew it was Dagger because he was talking as he walked over to the chair he sat in the day before. He sat down and put his elbows on his knees so he could be closer to the ground when he talked to me. He started in by telling me I was the worst kind of junkie.

I would be able to tell you I knew what he was talking about, but I only had that one experience at the strip club with drugs. I knew why he was saying all those things about me, but he was referring to the other me. I listened to him tell me how much of a scumbag I was, and of course he gave me examples. Such as the time I sold him all my furniture or my house. The lowest of the low was when I told him he could have my wife for a night. Then he went on and on about how he had taken her from me after only one night. It just showed how much of a pussy I was. I knew he was saying all these things to try and get a rise out of me.

Luckily, he didn't know he wasn't talking about me. It was kind of hard to get a rise out of me since he was referring to my worse half. He told me how he started making Anna hook on the corner for some extra money. Then he went into the drug business. This is where I became quite interested in the story. I found out exactly how this all came about in the first place.

It turns out; my reflection had started dabbling in drugs in college. Dagger was just a peon in his gang back then. Dagger and I had hooked up at a party in my sophomore year of college. I was smoking a joint on a couch surrounded by a couple of freshman girls who were trying to enlighten themselves through chemical enhancement. The hockey team at University of Illinois in Champaign-Urbana was throwing the party. Dagger was invited down there from Chicago by one of the players. I guess Dagger had begun to sell this guy weed in large quantities. Dagger was looking for new customers for his new heroin business.

I heard him tell me all about me being a total fiend for the stuff. He told me he put out a line for me and watch me snort it up and then run for the bathroom where I spent the rest of the night throwing up in the toilet. By morning, Dagger was staying at my apartment. He started using it as his base of operations for his thriving heroin business. The college kids were really enjoying having the amenities of the big city in that small college town.

The whole time Dagger told me his story; I was amazed at how similar the story was to my own memories. I remembered the party he was talking about. It was the hockey team that threw it. The guys I knew lived on the first floor of my apartment building. They would practice at weird hours of the night, like 2:00 AM, weird. Anyway, they would call me after they got home from the ice rink. I would always be the first to be invited. I would show up for an hour or so, but then head back upstairs because I usually had an early class scheduled.

I remembered the night he talked about when I spent it in the bathroom throwing up all night. It wasn't because I tried heroin for the first time; instead, it was right after my second date with Anna. We had gone out for some seafood and I got food poisoning before I even made it to the party. Then it all became clear to me. I knew Dagger. The whole time, my reflection talked about wanting to find this guy on my side, and I knew him.

I called out his first name. I got the meanest look I had ever seen in someone else's eyes. He looked at Visshes and nodded his head in my direction. One second, I was having my two worlds come together, and the next moment I felt a steel toe boot break my nose. I immediately started crying and wheezing. Blood poured out of my face all over the carpet. I could feel the throbbing in my face, and I could see my nose was bent and broken. I tried to get up but was helpless under the weight of Visshes on top of me.

Dagger looked at me and then asked me how I knew his real name. He sat back in his chair and stared at me really hard. I started thinking about how I could save this situation. I knew Dagger because he was one of my roommates in college. He was a real smart black kid who was able to overcome growing up in the ghetto of Chicago's West Side. He had put on a lot of weight and grew out his hair and beard, but it was Dagger, or how I knew him, Yarbrough Hunter.

Even though my face was full of blood and I couldn't breathe very well, I was starting to get a renewed vigor with the situation I was in. I told Dagger to tell his buddy to let me up, so I could at least breathe. I mean how he was going to get his money if I drowned in my own blood. He thought about it and then nodded his head in agreement. He told me to stay on the floor and tossed me one of the towels I threw me on the bed. I put it on my nose as I sat up. I slid my body over to the dresser and rested my back right below the television. Visshes pulled up the other chair and placed his 9mm Glock on his lap.

Trust me when I say that the gun's presence allowed me to never think about trying something sneaky. I just wanted off the floor so I could elevate my head and stop the bleeding. Dagger asked me how I knew his name. He said he never told me his real name. Then the questions about whether or not I was a cop started. I laughed that off, because it wasn't true. I knew I couldn't tell him he was my roommate in college on the other side. I also couldn't tell him his reflection wasn't doing very good. He was a smart kid but his mom got sick when we were seniors. He headed back to Chicago, and the last I heard he was working in some factory for a little more than minimum wage. A few of my college buddies that I still spoke with, always would ask about him, but I hadn't talked to him in a couple of years.

I was amazed at how similar the two worlds were, and yet they were totally different. I had to think of some great story to save my ass. Finally, I had a brainstorm of ideas. I started with telling him how Anna had told me his name. He asked me when I had seen her last, and I told her at the strip club. His eyes got really big, and then he laughed at me. He told Visshes that would be their next stop. Anna had taken off one night and disappeared. She was his property and he was going to claim it after I paid him.

The story kept him from asking any more questions about what I really knew. It also gave me some extra time. I looked at the clock and saw that it was 11:26 AM. I was very curious to know how I was doing on the other side. I prayed that he was getting the money and everything was going to pan out. I didn't know how much more tolerance to pain I was going to be able to handle.

Dagger finally stopped telling me stories from the past, but didn't stop calling me a junkie scumbag. He also liked reminding me of how I sold my wife to him for a bag of dope. Even if it was a really big bag, and that is when he asked where his money was. I reminded him of how he had given me until noon to pay him. He laughed at me, and told me; I must have thought he was the stupidest motherfucker in the universe. I did think that, but I wasn't going to agree with him out loud. My nose had slowed down in the bleeding enough for me to remove the towel from my face.

I tried to tell Dagger I needed some more time and he just laughed at me. He had come to collect because he knew I was going to skip out. He thought I was the stupidest junkie he had ever met. He figured I would have been gone already. I should have been gone already, but my reflection is not the brightest bulb in my head.

Dagger asked me where the money was, and I told him I had not gotten it yet. Then he asked me where it was, and I told him it was in the bank. That got him laughing, since he knew I was broke, and I had given him all my worldly possessions for heroin. I guess I was dealing the stuff for a while, but my habit got the best of me, and I ended up being my best customer. In the drug business, this is the worst thing for a dealer to be. I did not know this but I was learning a lot about something Economics 101 terms, "The Underground Economy." I had learned about it in college, but I was getting some hands-on training here.

He knew I didn't have a bank account, and I knew I did but there was no money in it over here. I tried to stall for some more time. That didn't go over very well because as soon as I started to ramble Dagger stood up with a calm demeanor. He walked over to me and kneeled down next me. He looked me straight in the eyes and told me my time was up. He said my time was up yesterday, but he liked to play games. He figured he could give me another day and watch me squirm like a bug. Visshes was parked across the street the whole time. I didn't know this because I was too busy sleeping off the Vicodin. Since I never left, Dagger figured I was lying to him.

Dagger held out his hand and Visshes put his gun into his hand. Dagger loaded a shell into the chamber and in an instant, I saw a blinding light and a sharp pain in my right kneecap. I screamed out in pain, and almost passed out. I wish I would have because I knew I would wake up in my own bed. But Dagger smacked me in the face to keep me awake. The weird thing about pain is it keeps you alive for longer than you want to be alive. It is a strong motivator. Not the motivator I was looking for at the time but a motivator nonetheless. Blood poured out of my leg all over the carpet. I clutched my upper thigh as I felt a surge of pain throughout my whole leg. The pain was so intense I almost passed out again.

My vision blurred and then focused on Dagger breaking something under my nose. A few seconds later I was wide awake. I figured out later he planned on doing this to me, I mean he brought smelling salt with him. Dagger motioned for Visshes to grab the other towels off the bed. Dagger gave the gun back to Visshes and then tossed the towels in my lap. He stood up and told me to wrap up my leg. I told him he could take a flying fuck. He kicked me in the side of the head, and laughed at my negative attitude.

I knew I still had to buy some time until the money could be withdrawn. I grabbed the towels and wrapped up the bullet wound as best as I could. Truthfully, it wasn't that good. The towels became blood soaked rather quickly. Dagger opened the door of the room and walked outside.

Visshes held the gun at me just to make sure I wouldn't try anything. I thought about yelling for help, but I knew that would only make it worse on me, and not better. So, I kept my mouth shut and watched as Dagger came back from the parking lot. He was carrying a roll of duct tape and a skullcap. He pushed me over with his boot and then put his other foot on the back of my leg where the bullet had exited. I screamed in pain and tried to not cry, but the tears rolled from my eyes as I rolled over onto my stomach. Dagger told me to put my hands behind my back. I did exactly as I was told.

I felt the duct tape being wrapped around my wrists. He rolled me back over onto my back. He started telling me how I deserve everything I got coming. In my mind, that meant there was still more to come, but I didn't care. The pain was excruciating that I wanted to die. Or the other thought I had was to pass out. At least that way I could end up on the other side. Every time I closed my eyes, I would get kicked, punched, or pistol-whipped. After being hit in the nose a few times I finally quit trying to fall asleep or pass out.

Dagger began to duct tape my feet together, and I thought about kicking him in the face, but the pain in my leg was so intense I couldn't even feel it below my hip. I could feel the pain, but it was the like the leg just disappeared off my brain's radar. The other leg would have given him a nice surprise right square in his nose, but then Visshes would probably have shot me in the head without hesitation. I was kind of in a pickle as my grandfather used to say.

Dagger finished subduing me with the hog tie. The final piece of my new wardrobe was rolled down over my face. The last thing I saw was the shitty grin Dagger gave me as I was enveloped in darkness from the dark cloth of the skullcap over my face. I thought it was the end of it all, but then I felt the pressure of tape being tape around my head. It wasn't loose either; I could feel the pressure in my face. The only good thing about it was that I think it stopped my nose from continuing to bleed.

I was lying there silent and motionless. It was the time I needed to collect my thoughts. My vision was blocked and I had the pain to keep me focused. Without the eyes, your other senses take over. I was able to feel my heartbeat, and it was a rapid beat. I felt the pulse of the blood throughout my head, especially where the wounds were fresh. I came to the conclusion that they would just put a bullet in my head as their next plan of action. I was wrong about that thought, but I tried to figure out what else they could do to me that would cause me more pain than I was already in.

I heard them discussing their next move. It turns out I wasn't going to die at that moment, even though the pleasant thought of death relaxed me. They had decided to take me back to my house, which was actually Dagger's house. I felt my body being lifted off of the ground. They carried me outside, and the only reason I knew this is because the cold air was a great feeling. I was sweating before Dagger put the skullcap over my face, but since then the heavy cloth was causing me to drip sweat. I could only imagine how the fabric must have looked like from the outside.

I heard a door of a vehicle open, and then I was tossed onto the carpet. I figured I was in the back of the SUV but I couldn't tell. I hit the carpet so hard I felt the burn of the carpeting slide across my exposed skin on my arms. Not that it mattered much; I find it funny that rug burns were the least of my worries. I heard the door slam next to me, and then two other doors opened up on the driver's side. I assumed it was the driver's side because obviously someone had to drive my transportation.

I know I am kind of being funny about the whole situation but as I think back to it all in my mind, it wasn't that bad. I find it comical that they were kidnapping a real person. They had no idea they were hurting the wrong person. Revenge is a powerful tool that human beings have tried to master over the centuries. But the truth is we are human and therefore all our thoughts are flawed to some extent. This is proven when they tried to exact their revenge on me. I wasn't the guy that screwed them, and that is why I look back at this experience and laugh at myself. Hindsight is 20/20, just like I had said earlier.

At this point, I really don't care who believes me and who doesn't. I got the scars to prove it. So, there I was rolling in the back of some vehicle. I was going to try and sleep but I lost the power of blood loss or shock. I was becoming more and more energized. I kept thinking about having to survive. I wanted to live to see Anna. I wanted my routine back. I thought I like the excitement of my world switching. But the truth is; it loses its glamour after enough physical pain.

The bumps in the road were rough on me. Every time the vehicle bounced, I bounced. I would cry out in pain or sigh really loud, and afterwards I would hear Dagger and Visshes laughing at me. I tried my hardest to "man up" as my father used to say, but it was really difficult considering the circumstances. I wished I knew the direction of travel that we took, but I was totally lost in the darkness of my head covering. I definitely respect blind people today.

It felt like an eternity being in the dark. At first, I felt the pain from a rather large pothole, and I realized there was only one hole that size that was unavoidable. The pothole in question was on block right behind my house. I felt the vehicle turn and then I heard the rumbling echo of the exhaust on the walls of a garage. The rumble was loud which told me we had made it to our destination. I tried to get comfortable for a second because I knew I would be moved in a few seconds. I heard the doors open, and then slam shut. I could hear Dagger and Visshes discussing something outside of the vehicle.

I tried to stop my breathing hoping to hear what they were talking about. Then the door opened, and I felt a fist hit me in the stomach. I curled upwards, but that only intensified the pain in my leg. I only fell back to the carpet with a thud.

I heard Visshes let out a chuckle and tell me how I would be dead already if it was up to him. I saw a chance for a little retribution of my own. I told him he couldn't do shit because he was Dagger's flunky. He would never cross Dagger, and therefore I was untouchable. Visshes reaction was exactly the thing I needed. I got punched two more times in the stomach, which I was prepared for, but the third shot was to the face. That one hurt really bad. I was becoming a tender piece of meat after all the tenderizing.

The thing I learned at the moment was that I had touched a nerve with Visshes. The old saying, "Absolute power corrupts absolutely" holds true. This is especially true for the men who always served in second place, look at the Devil and God if you need an excellent example. Visshes was a puppet of Dagger but anyone could see he was a quiet guy. I learned a lot about the quiet guy when I still owned my business. My partner was the quiet type. He was always thinking about the big picture. He could formulate great ideas and plans if I left him alone to himself for a few hours. It was scary sometimes because I knew there were other things going on his head. I saw the same look in Visshes' eyes the day before when I first met him and Dagger. I couldn't see that now, but I knew what those eyes were hiding.

After Visshes got done beating me up some more, there was a long silence. I could hear him breathing but he didn't speak. I was beginning to get nervous. I didn't like silence all that much, especially when there were other people around me. I felt like the outsider, because my brain didn't get all worked up unless I was by myself. Usually, when there were other people around, I liked to converse. However, this was not the time to say anything else. Visshes was in a violent mood obviously, and I was getting very sore all over my body.

A few minutes passed and then I heard Dagger's voice from the other side of the garage. I felt my body being lifted up out of the vehicle. I heard the garage door closing as I was being carried on what I assumed to be Visshes' shoulder. I heard the door of the garage slam shut behind me, and then Dagger told Visshes to bring me downstairs into the basement. I felt the taped skullcap being pulled off my head as I bounced on the shoulder. It didn't come off very easily, and Dagger was cussing at me for it. He finally gave up and left it on my head.

We went down a bunch of steps and I can tell you that every one of them hurt me. I felt us level out, and then I was slammed down into a chair. My hands took most of the damage. I swore out loud. I got smacked in the back of the head and was told to shut up. I felt some handcuffs being placed around my ankles, and my wrists. I was already hogtied with duct tape, and now I was handcuffed around my ankles, wrists, and those were chained together to the floor. I could barely move. Dagger pulled my head backwards over the chair and I heard the tape ripping over my face. The skullcap came off my face and I had to squint because the lights were very bright. I looked around and saw concrete walls with mattresses lining the walls around me. I was sitting in a steel chair. I looked down and saw an O ring in the concrete floor where the chain holding my wrists and ankles was connected. The O ring was familiar, it was an exact replica of the ring bolted to the wall in the jail cell I had found myself in a few nights earlier. That night seemed like an eternity ago, but here I was finding myself chained to concrete, but always in a new and exciting position.

Dagger came out from behind me and looked at me with a smirk. He was really enjoying the pain I was in. He even asked me if I was feeling the pain. I nodded my head in agreement, and then he laughed and punched me in the bullet hole in my leg. I screamed out in pain. He told me how nobody was going to hear me so scream all I want.

I didn't hesitate to take him up on the offer. The pain was becoming unbearable, I was moving around in the chair like a little kid does when he has to use the bathroom. Dagger pulled up a chair and sat in it. He told Visshes to go make himself something to eat. Visshes didn't hesitate to follow orders, and that is when I told him to make me some eggs and bacon. With a side of toast, I added at the end for a little sarcasm. Dagger laughed, but the look on Visshes' face told me he wasn't even laughing on the inside.

I didn't care anymore about these two scumbags. I knew I was going to get Dagger his money and if I could just find a mirror, I would be looking really good. Dagger started telling me his thoughts again about me and my decisions to screw him over. I tried to speak periodically, but I was shut up with a punch, kick, or slap. It all depended on how sarcastic the comments were that came out of my mouth.

I finally realized that the only way I was going to get out this situation was to make Dagger believe I had to go somewhere to get the money. I would not be here today to tell this story if I didn't get out of that basement. Dagger asked me how it felt to be back in my house. He asked me if I liked what he did with the place. I laughed at that, because he obviously had tortured other people in this basement. I was familiar with it; it was my basement after all.

Dagger finally felt rested I guess, because he went upstairs and left me a bloody mess. I don't know how much time had passed because the room I was in didn't have any windows. It was the utility room on my side. I used this place to store stuff, such as paint, tools, and whatever else a man is supposed to have.

Dagger and Visshes came back downstairs. They were laughing about something when they came into the room. Although I didn't know what it was, I got the feeling it wasn't going to be good for me. Dagger sat back down and I saw that Visshes was carrying a milk crate full of tools, water, rags, a six pack of Budweiser in the bottles, and a bunch of other stuff I couldn't see. Let me just tell you that everything in the crate was especially for me, which didn't make me feel very good on the inside.

Dagger grabbed the milk carton they had filled with water. He told me he didn't want me to die just yet, so I was going to get a reprieve for a little while. I opened up the carton and let me drink some of the water. Now I would have spit it into his face, but I did have to stay alive at all costs. After I had my fill of water, he started pouring it over my face and leg. I watched the bloody water begin to collect in pools on the floor. Then he pulled out a pair of scissors, which I thought was for pain, but he instead cut the fabric around my bullet wound. He then went back to cleaning it out with the water. It felt great. It was like an oasis after someone gets lost in the desert for a couple of days. The water was refreshing, and it relaxed me. Not for long of course, but it did relax me.

Dagger finished playing doctor and then reached over and grabbed a beer. He popped the top and offered me some as a joke. I wasn't biting though. I was trying to anticipate his next move. He laughed to himself and told Visshes to have a beer. He said something like this is going to be fun. Or something along those lines, and then put the beer down, untied my shoe on the other leg without the bullet hole, and then proceeded to make comments about my stinky feet as he cut off my sock with the scissors. He took another swig of beer, and then grabbed a pair of pruning shears out of the crate. I would have loved to tell you he took his time, but he didn't. He reached down and snipped of my pinky toe. I started crying immediately. I had just started to get used to pain from everything else, and I watched as the blood squirted out of my foot all over his shoes. He busted out laughing while I screamed in horror. I asked why he was doing this, why couldn't he just kill me and get it over with.

I started to tell him I was going to get him his money. This slowed him for a second, and then he asked me to tell him where the money was. He would send Visshes to get it and I could then go on my merry way. I knew he was full of shit, and he thought the same of me, but I was telling the truth. I was beginning to understand that if and when I paid him that would be the moment I would die.

I put my head back on the chair and cried out loud forever. Dagger and Visshes sipped on their beers as they watched me squirm. No matter how hard I tried to free myself it was useless. The pain increased the more I moved, so I finally just stopped fighting it, and let the tears roll down my cheeks. I started thinking about everything that had happened to me in the days leading up to this.

Dagger gave me reprieve from the torture. He let me sit and bleed for long periods of time, and then would punch or kick me. I think he just wanted to make sure I stayed alive so he could get his money's worth. Even though I wasn't the guy he should have been trying to collect from, but I was the guy paying from both sides. I was trying to get him my money, and yet here I was being tortured for not having in time. My anger increased with every passing moment. It was not building up because of Dagger, it was directed towards my reflection, and ultimately towards myself.

Dagger was getting bored with punching and kicking me; he even said he was getting tired of beating me up. He wanted to see me scream. He started telling me he was going to make me tell him where the money was. He didn't believe I even had it, but he wasn't going to let me die until he was sure of it. I welcomed the thought of telling him where the money was coming from, but he wouldn't have believed me. He probably would have killed me right then and there.

I think I might have passed out for a few moments but I can't be sure. I thought the whole time if I fell asleep or passed out then I would wake up in my world. I don't know if I was just starting to go into shock and my mind was shutting down, but I was still awake, or if I actually did pass out. I do remember opening my eyes and seeing him with the shears in his hand. I eyed him suspiciously as he stood up from his chair. He told Visshes to leave, and waited for him to go all the way up the staircase before he approached me. He walked around behind me and made sure I couldn't see him.

I felt the cold metal on my left forefinger. I screamed out in pain as the shears began to slice through my skin. It didn't cut right away. It was a slow cut, and when he reached the bone right by the center joint, I felt a lot of pressure in my hand. The pain was so intense I gritted my teeth. I felt a tooth snap under the pressure in my mouth, and a second later I heard my finger fall to the floor. You are probably wondering how I heard my finger hit the floor, but for some reason my senses were becoming bionic. I felt the blood squirting out of my finger in rhythm with my heartbeat.

I could hear Dagger laughing at me from behind. I laid my head back on the chair and tried to see him. I told him I was going to kill him and there would be no end to my revenge if he didn't kill me in this basement. I would come back from the dead. I would haunt him until his death, and when he left this plane of existence, I would torture him for eternity. I would have sold my soul to the Devil for an eternity of hell, as long I was able to have 24 hours with him.

He found it really funny, and I tried to squirm out of the chair. I bounced the chair up and down on the concrete trying to break free. The pain was increasing all over my body. My toe had stopped bleeding, the bullet hole was starting to clot, and my nose was caked with so much blood, it hurt when I tried to talk because I could feel my skin tightening from the caked blood. I tried screaming again for a long time, but it was no use. I knew that nobody outside could hear me, and if they could they would not have done anything about it.

I finally surrendered; I began to tell Dagger that the money was back at the hotel. I would only show him where it was over there. No matter how much he tortured me I would never tell him the exact location. I would die first before I would do that. He might have believed me and he might not have, but the torture stopped. He left me alone to cry while he went upstairs. Thoughts about what to do ran through my mind. I had to get out of the basement somehow. I also needed to find a mirror. I hoped my reflection had gotten the money. I was kicking myself in the ass for not allowing him to kill Dagger like he had told me he wanted to do.

I bowed my head on my chest. I shut my eyes because I was getting very nauseous looking at all my wounds. I tried to concentrate on a story that would free me temporarily. If I could convince him to let me go back to hotel to show him where the money was, then I just might have a chance at surviving. I waited for what seemed like hours for Dagger to return. I heard the door upstairs open and then the footsteps on the stairs, and finally he appeared in the doorway. He asked me if I was feeling better. He told me he sent Visshes to look for the money. If he found it, then he would kill me right away instead of making me suffer. If Visshes didn't find it, then he was going to torture me until I died of blood loss. I tried to explain he would never get the money if he didn't take me back to the hotel. He laughed at me, but I got him thinking, I could see it in his eyes. Then I told him I needed some kind of medical treatment or I would die of blood loss before he ever touched one penny of my money. He stared at me long and hard after I said that. I mean, how does a man that is in a situation like this, lie?

He left me alone for another ten minutes or so, and then I heard two sets of feet walking down the stairs. I figured Visshes had returned. I knew it would be empty-handed. Dagger appeared in the doorway with a very familiar face. He was holding Anna by the back of her head. He asked me if I remember her, or was I too much of a junkie to care about my wife. I didn't care about her, and I didn't know her. She looked like Anna, but my reflection looked like me, and we were not the same person. Anna must not have liked the look on my face because she started to screaming and swearing at me. I tried to understand some of things she was angry about, but they were all situations, places, and things I was not around to know about.

Dagger told her he wanted her to wash out my cuts and bandage me up real nice, so I could live a few more days. Anna looked at him and that is when she realized how much damage had been done to me. I could see anger turn to sympathy in her eyes. When she first appeared in the doorway, she must not have noticed what had really happened to me. Dagger told her to run upstairs like a good little whore and grab the bag of supplies off of the table. She didn't hesitate and ran back up the stairs. Dagger turned to me and laughed at me. He told me she loved him a hell of a lot more than she ever loved me. I laughed at that, and told him he was right. I was starting to want to play his game. I told him I got more money from him for her than she was worth. I laughed out loud and then watched him grab the crate of torture tools and disappear upstairs.

A few minutes passed and then Anna returned with a grocery bag full of gauze, alcohol, tape, a milk jug full of water, needle and thread, and a few other items that looked really pleasant to me. She dumped everything out on the floor next to the wall, since the floor around me was one big pool of blood. I didn't know how I was still alive, but I was grateful I had gotten some time to recover. I didn't know how much time, but it was time nonetheless.

She started by cleaning all my wounds with the water and rags. Every part of my body that she touched I squirmed in pain. We didn't talk at first. I felt a little uncomfortable being around my wife, but I knew it wasn't really my wife. I finally told her I loved her. She stopped cleaning out my bullet wound and looked me in the eyes. She started crying and then put her head in her hands. She then wiped her eyes and punched me in the hole in my leg. I screamed out and called her a bitch. She laughed at me. She then said how that sounded more like me. She told me how she hoped Dagger would kill me, and if he didn't maybe she should.

I realized I should have just kept my mouth shut. I also realized that she hated me, but I could see a little love left in her. I know

I had probably hurt this woman really bad. I had sold her to my drug dealer, and he turned her into a whore. I didn't know how my reflection was able to live with what he did, but I am sure it took a lot of drugs to deal with it on a daily basis. I couldn't imagine doing anything like that to Anna. My brain started to tell me there was an angle to work here. I knew I had to be me in order for her to gain some confidence in me. If I could get her on my side, then maybe I could get out of here.

I told her we shouldn't talk, and if she could please finish stitching me up in silence I would not mind at all. She nodded her head in agreement. I knew she didn't want to hear me talk either. I didn't know this woman, and I had no idea how to win over her heart. I watched her slowly stitch up my wound on my leg. My nose was a lost cause, and she finally told me in order to stop the bleeding on my finger and toe she was going to have to burn the wounds close. I shook my head in disbelief. After bowing my head and letting out a sigh of regret, I agreed. She pulled a lighter out of her pants pocket and told me to brace myself. I gritted my teeth again, and shut my eyes. I put my head back to brace it against the chair. I heard the flint spark and then I began to feel the heat on my toe. I started to smell the flesh burning, and I writhed in pain. She tried to hold my foot in place, but I know it must have been difficult. She finished with my foot and stood up.

I opened my eyes and it still felt like my toe was being burned, but she had closed the wound. She walked around behind me and told me to brace myself once again. I put my head forward against my chest and felt my finger being fried by a Bic lighter. I screamed out in pain, and then it was all over. I ran my middle finger over the wound and felt the flesh all bubbled up from the flame. I could only imagine how it must have looked.

She walked back and stood in front of me. I looked into her eyes and saw the pain of a lost and tortured soul. After a moment of the uncomfortable silence, I finally said thank you, and then asked if she had anything to kill the pain. She laughed at me, and told me, I should know better. She reached into her pocket and pulled out an Altoids canister. She opened up the case and pulled two small pink pills from the box. She grabbed the jug of water and helped me swallow the pills. I asked what they were, and she looked at me funny. She asked me what was going on. I wasn't acting like myself, and it was not normal for me to not know what Xanex looked like.

I tried to tell her I wasn't the same Jack she knew. She found that funny, and I then I realized she was a little slower than my Anna. My Anna was well educated and acted like an adult; this Anna was like a fragile child. She looked into my eyes for a long time and then said I wasn't Jack. I could see she was getting frightened and was about to run upstairs. I called out her name and told her I could explain everything if she just would stop and listen. She stopped at the door, but she didn't turn to face me.

I began to tell her how I was Jack but not the Jack she knew. I tried to explain it all like I was Jack's twin brother. It was the only way I was able to get my point across. After about five minutes of explaining how I needed to get out of the basement and find Jack, she finally turned to face me. I could tell she was crying. Her eyes were all red, her face puffy, and she was trying desperately to believe me. Let's face it; nobody believes the truth, even when it is staring you in the face.

I told her that Jack and I had figured out how to pay Dagger off. I told her I needed to get back to the motel as soon as possible. She told me she couldn't cross Dagger again. She had nothing. She needed to stay with him. He was taking care of her. I asked her about the incident at the strip club. She laughed at me, and told me her and Dagger were fighting. She told me she had to do that once and a while just to feel needed inside. I felt really bad, but I knew this woman was the only thing that could save my life.

Finally, I broke down, and started to talk about Jack. She became really interested when I told her how he reacted after I told him I saw her at the strip club. I tried to finish telling her more and more, but I started to fade in and out of consciousness. I did my best to stay awake. Finally, I realized it was time for me to go back to my side. Maybe I could fix the situation that way. The last thing I said to Anna was how I needed to get back to the motel room to meet Jack. He was waiting for me. She asked me what my name was, since we were brothers and all. She was catching on, but my eyes rolled into the back of my head, and everything went black and silent.

CHAPTER 8

I opened my eyes slowly expecting to see my bedroom. My heart and stomach both had pain when I realized I was still in the basement chained to the chair. I looked around the room and couldn't comprehend why I was still here. I tried to break free of the chains, hoping some divine intervention had taken place while I was knocked out. I felt a lot worse and my whole body ached. I looked at my leg and noticed the bullet hole had re-opened. It was not that bad, but I could see blood soaking the gauze. I got really angry and started squirming around in the chair. My efforts were futile and useless. I was chained and I couldn't be freed without a key.

I couldn't tell what time it was and I didn't know what was going to happen, but I was tired, sore, angry, and helpless. I started screaming hoping someone would hear me. I didn't care if it was Dagger either. I just wanted to get out. Whether that meant death or suicide, I didn't care. I heard the upstairs door open and then the footsteps down the stairs.

Dagger walked into the room. He asked me if I had a pleasant sleep. He told me he had Anna fix me up with a shot of dope while I was passed out. He wanted me well rested for today. I asked him what time it was, and he told me it was around 9:30 AM. I tried to think about how long I had been chained to the chair. It had been almost a full day. I asked if he was going to kill me today. I almost pleaded for him to do it. He laughed at me and called me names. He told me he wasn't finished yet. He wanted me to be the example. When people would think about screwing him in the future, they could think of me. He said I would be immortalized in the memories of all dope fiends.

I looked at him square in the eye, and then my instincts took over. I told him he was the sorriest dope dealer I had ever met. His product was garbage, and his attitude would get him killed in the near future. He laughed for a split second and then realized I was serious. He got angry and I saw the rage in his eyes. He left the room, stomped upstairs, and then I heard him coming back down a few seconds later.

He appeared in the room with the crate of torture devices. He walked over to me and pulled his pistol. He told me I wasn't going to be that guy who took him out. Without hesitating after his last word, he sent a bullet through my leg. The bullet pierced my leg within inches of my other wound. I tried to kick and move, but all I could do was scream. The bullet came out the other side and bounced off a bare part of the wall where the mattresses didn't cover. The bullet ricocheted off the wall into the chain on the floor.

I felt my feet had been freed, and I reacted to the sudden freedom. I kicked him as hard as I could, with my good leg, in the balls. He immediately grabbed his crotch and tried to get away from me. I didn't hesitate and kicked him repeatedly in the balls until he finally fell over from the pain. He had dropped his gun, and if my hands were not handcuffed behind my back, I would have grabbed it. I jumped up from the chair and pulled on the chain that was still connected to my wrists. I started running for the stairs. I heard the clinking of the steel links banging on the floor behind me as I ran. I flew up the stairs three at a time. I heard him say something to me but I couldn't make it out. I had tunnel vision, and my only focus was the door to the upstairs.

He had left it open, thinking back I don't know how I would have been able to open it if he hadn't. I flew up into the kitchen and glanced into the front room. Anna was watching television. I yelled for her, and she was so scared she jumped up and screamed for Dagger. I told her to shut up, and get me out of there. She hesitated for a few seconds, and then I told her I would make sure she had enough money to disappear for the rest of her life if she helped me. I still hadn't heard Dagger coming up the stairs, but my heart was beating so fast, I couldn't concentrate, but I wasn't feeling any more pain. The adrenaline that was pumping through my veins was giving me freedom from the pain. I didn't know how long it was going to last like that. I was able to lift my leg slightly to move around. She came running at me and I flinched thinking she was going to hit me. She grabbed a set of car keys off the table and grabbed my arm. We headed for the garage door. I heard Dagger yelling as he was making his way up the stairs as the garage door slammed shut.

She jumped in the SUV that was parked in the garage. I saw the garage door begin to open and then I heard the engine start up as I hobbled to the closest door, which happened to be the back door on the driver's side. I jumped in and she peeled out the open garage door into the alley. I watched as Dagger came running into the garage. He fired two or three shots at us while we flew down the alley. The last shot shattered the glass on the back door. Anna and I were not hit, and I sat up to look out the busted window. I saw Dagger run back into the garage. I knew it wasn't going to be long before he would come after us.

Anna asked me where we were headed. I told her to go to the motel. After we made the left on Elston Avenue off of Pulaski, I tried to climb into the front seat. I was bleeding all over the leather interior. I finally was able to straighten up in the front, but the pain in my body increased every second. I started to feel woozy, and Anna kept shaking me to make sure I was awake. She kept telling me she wanted me to live. I thought she was being considerate, but she just wanted her money.

I finally had the clearest thought of my entire life. I reached for the sun visor, and pulled it down. There it was a mirror! I opened the plastic cover and I looked at my swollen face. My red hair was all stuck together with blood. The freckles on my face were no longer visible because of the distorted face I had from all the beatings. The funny thing is I started beating myself up long before Dagger ever did any damage. My nose was deformed, and it looked unfixable. My left eye was swollen shut, which I hadn't even noticed. The other eye was blood red where the whites were supposed to be. I must have popped the blood vessels from all the pressure on my face. I looked nothing like I did when I woke up the day before. I started laughing at myself, and then he said something.

"Where the fuck have you been?" He said.

"What about you?" I replied.

"You look bad." He said.

I laughed at his joke, but I needed to get serious really fast. "Did you get the money?" I asked in a hurried tone.

"Yeah, I got it. I was on my way from the bank back to the house when I decided to stop on the West Side to buy some dope. I was going through withdrawals, and I didn't think I could make back to the house." He said.

"Are you fucking kidding me?" I said.

"Nope, but right after I scored the dope, there was a drive-by shooting. Two bullets came through the passenger side of the car and hit me in the leg. I lost control of the car and it flipped. When I finally woke up, I was in a hospital missing a toe and a finger. Not to mention I broke our nose. What about you? How did it happen on your side?" He asked.

"Dagger showed up. I should have let you kill that motherfucker." I replied.

We both laughed about the situation and then discussed what our next move should be. I knew that Dagger would be on our trail in no time. I had to act fast, and I couldn't be without a mirror. I thought about the motel since that is where we were headed. Then I thought about Dagger probably heading there first. For all I knew, Visshes might have already been there. I told Anna to turn on Foster Avenue and head for LaBagh Woods. I knew we could chill there for a few minutes. As long as Dagger was not heading down Foster, he would never see the truck. The trees did an excellent job of natural camouflage. I knew this from when I was kid and used to hang out there with all my friends from the neighborhood.

I looked at Anna for a second then told her I needed a few minutes to think. I told her I would appreciate her not saying anything to me. I needed to talk to myself in my head, and if I was distracted, then it would just take longer to figure out what we were going to do.

"You with my Anna?" He asked me.

"Yeah, you with my Anna?" I asked in reply.

"Yep, weird huh? Two totally different women! I got to get back. I got the money at the house. You have to go back to the motel." He said.

"I can't, Dagger will be heading there." I said.

"It's cool if he is, that's the whole point with the money, right?" He asked.

I thought about it for a minute, and he was right. Dagger needed to be dealt with, and I wasn't the guy to do it. He would be able to do more damage to him if I was on my side. I think that was proven earlier in the day. This world was not mine, and I wasn't mean enough for this lifestyle.

"I told Anna I would give her enough money to disappear. Keep my promise for me. I am going to let her off here in LaBagh woods. Come back for her if we make it out of this alive." I said, even though I was very unsure of the future.

"Look, everything is going to work out. I will take care of Anna; I have been avoiding it for years anyway. Plus, I have finally gotten the heroin out of my system. I couldn't do the dope I bought yesterday because of the drive-by. It has been almost three days since I fixed up. The withdrawals were bad, but I had morphine at the hospital." He said.

"Hospital? When were you at the hospital?" I asked.

"Right after I was shot, I lost control of the car and flipped it. I was rushed to the emergency room where they patched up all my wounds." He said nonchalant.

"I have been over getting stitched up by your girl, chained to a chair, and you were in the hospital getting morphine for the pain? Now that is some bullshit." I said angrily.

"Sorry man, your side is not so bad, kind of boring, but nice. I still miss my side, so I don't want to come back here ever again." He told me.

"You took the words right out of my mouth. I will meet you at the motel." I said as I closed the mirror and turned to look at Anna.

I explained to her that she needed to get away from Dagger. I told her she was going to have to get out of the truck. I would come back for her, but first I had to go pay Dagger his money. She didn't believe me at first, but then I told her I was going to face Dagger, which wasn't a smart idea, but it had to be done. She started screaming and yelling at me about things I knew nothing about. Everything she said to me must have been about things that were going on between her and my other half. I finally got fed up and reached over and opened her door. I was in a lot of pain but I managed to push her out of the truck. She tried to fight me, but I could tell she was as tired of living as I was. I climbed over into the driver's seat and looked out the window. I told her everything would be all right, put the truck into gear and drove through the parking lot towards Foster Avenue.

I drove as fast as I could towards the motel. I tried to think about how the situation was going to play out. I couldn't fathom anything but probably dying from a gunshot. I knew Dagger wanted me dead before I tried to crush his manhood. I was flying down Elston Avenue. I could see the motel drawing closer, and then I knew I was going to have to park the truck around the block. The thought of walking on my legs was not settling well with me.

I parked the truck and limped towards the back of the Esquire. I slithered around the building and looked into the office. I didn't see anybody at the desk, and then peeked around the corner. I looked across the street into the diner's parking lot. It was empty. I looked up and down Milwaukee Avenue. I didn't see anything unusual. I was looking for a parked car with one or more people sitting in it. I couldn't tell because of the glare from the sun. I slithered towards my room. I tried the handle on the door, and it was locked. I checked my pockets but my key was gone. Dagger must have taken it when he sent Visshes out to find the money.

I took a step back and put my shoulder into the door. I hit it so hard I felt the pain in my fractured arm. The door didn't move, but I fell backwards and hit the pavement with my head breaking my fall. It took me a second to get my bearings. I was becoming lethargic. I knew I had lost a lot of blood. I rolled over onto my stomach and pushed myself off the ground. I stood up on my good leg. Even though I was missing a toe on that foot, the pain didn't compare to the fresh gunshot wound in my leg. I stood there and looked over my shoulder just to make sure nobody was sneaking up on me. The coast appeared to be clear, but I got the feeling I was being watched.

I finally decided that I needed to get into that room. I walked over to the window, and smashed my elbow through the glass. It shattered, and there was a shard of glass sticking out of my skin. I winced in pain and grabbed at the small piece of glass. I pulled it out and watched the blood seep from the small puncture. It wasn't as bad as I had been used to as of late. I began knocking out the other pieces of glass out of the window's frame. After I ran my hand across the metal frame to assure myself that I wouldn't get poked again, I lifted my body up onto the window sill. I lifted my bad leg with my arms to clear the other windowpane. I set it down inside the room, and then I lifted my other leg into the room. I tried really hard to not put pressure on the bad leg. That didn't work out to well.

I pushed the drapes out of the way, and fell into the room. Luckily nobody was in the room. I was a sitting duck behind that curtain. I wasn't very quiet because of my movement problems, and if Dagger or Visshes were sitting there when I emerged from the drapes, I probably would have dropped dead of a heart attack.

I looked around the room and saw that it had been ransacked. All the drawers and their contents were thrown everywhere I could see. I knew what had happened and it was not surprising in the least. I headed for the bathroom. I walked in and looked at myself. We had made it, and I was thankful. I leaned up on the sink and took the pressure off my legs. I was about to collapse, and I was not sure how much longer I would be conscious for. My eyes were becoming blurry. I was feeling dizzy, and I knew that if I didn't get some medical attention soon, I was not going to have to worry about Dagger, but instead my judgment day.

"How we going to do this? Dagger is not here." I said.

"Well, we have to transport this money to that side. There is a lot of money here. I fit it all into my pockets, socks, and waistline. So, now I need you to pull me through. I never told you how I did it. The key is to believe that there is another side to life." He said.

"I believe! Trust me on that." I replied.

"Well, just put your hands through and touch me. That is all you have to do." He said as he laughed.

"Really, I tried that before, it doesn't work." I said.

"Before, you still didn't believe in me. Now you do. Just try it." He said.

I felt kind of silly, but I reached towards the mirror, and my hands went through like it was jelly. I felt a cool breeze on the other side, and then I felt the fabric of his shirt. I touch his shoulders, and then he was beside me in the bathroom.

"See, this side has the power for that. I don't know why, I figured it out one day when I was high. Remember when we had that terrible cold last winter?" He asked.

"Yeah, I slipped in the bathroom and blacked out." I replied.

"Well, sort of, I actually pulled you through, and then you got hysterical so I knocked you out by pushing you into the bathtub." He said.

"I thought that was a dream?" I said.

"Nope, I am sorry, but I didn't mess with you for almost a whole year after that. I thought I was really high, and I wasn't going to tempt fate. But as this shit with Dagger got worse, I kind of had no choice. I mean if I died then so would you. So, I figured I would see what your side was like. Then I found out you had all that money. So, I saw a way out." He said.

"Look man, you need to go somewhere and get into a rehab or something. I am thinking the psych ward. I mean if I go then you go. We can chill out for a few months, let you get your bearings, and then we can try this again. Oh yeah, I passed out yesterday, why did I wake up over here?" I asked.

"I don't know. That is good question. I was thinking the same thing when I woke up in the hospital this morning. Did you take your pills yesterday?" He asked.

I started laughing out loud. I guess the pills did work, but it was kind of backwards. I was stuck over here for a night. It was a night that almost killed me.

"Well, this is it? I think you should get back to your side and enjoy the fireworks." He said.

"What fireworks? I won't be able to see anything, otherwise that would mean that Dagger would have to be in my house on my side." I replied. It was all beginning to make sense in my mind.

"You are right about that, but those are not the fireworks I am talking about. Just when you go back over there, try to hang onto that woman of yours. She is a great thing. I am going to try and keep Anna in my life over here, but I think it might be a hopeless dream of mine. One more favor, don't come back to a mirror until you open your front door to some unknown guests." He said.

"What the hell are you talking about? I am sick of being left in the dark. Tell me what did you do?" I asked.

"I am not going to tell you; just promise you won't go near a mirror." He said. I could tell he was adamant about it, so I left it alone. I knew he was not going to let anything happen to us, I mean we were in this together, life and limb; literally.

"I promise. Take care of yourself. Don't be afraid to talk to me either. I am just a mirror away." I laughed.

"Bad joke man, real bad." He said. "Now Go!"

I reached through the mirror and felt the cool breeze again. Except this time, it covered my whole body as I slipped through to the other side. I fell to the floor with a loud thud. I tried to get up, but it was becoming very hard to move. Anna had heard me fall and came running into the bathroom. She started getting hysterical at the sight of the bleeding gunshot in my leg. She started swearing she was going to sue the hospital, and I told to her to help me up. She helped me up and I was about to walk out of the bathroom, when I glanced over to the other side.

I saw Anna in the mirror, which meant Anna, had to be at the room.

"I told her to wait at the woods!" I said out loud.

"She can't stay away for me." He said in my head with a loud boisterous laugh. "Good luck, and remember no mirrors."

I told Anna to get me to bed as quickly as possible. She wanted to take me to the hospital, but I yelled at her to take me to the bedroom. I hobbled to my bed and then told her to get some wet towels, I needed to clean the wound and stop the bleeding and after watching the other Anna yesterday, I knew what had to be done.

Anna ran back into the bedroom with the towels. That is when there was a knock at the front door. She ran off to answer it, and I heard a lot of voices and commotion coming from the hallway. Anna ran back in and told me the U.S. Treasury department was here to speak with me. I was really confused. Two officers with the Treasury came into my bedroom.

They saw my gunshot wound, and immediately radioed for an ambulance. They started telling me it was going to be all right, I just needed to relax. Help was on its way. I found this to be pretty funny. I was the calmest guy in the room. They started telling me why they were there.

I had called them about a possible counterfeit money operation being run out of the house. They thought it was a joke at first, but then they had checked my records. They saw that I had withdrawn a lot of money from my accounts on Wall Street. I tried to tell them I had no idea what they were talking about, but they told me I was delirious. They had recorded my voice from my anonymous phone call. It would have been anonymous, but I guess I had talked for too long on the phone. It gave them a chance to trace the call.

I heard the sirens from the ambulance outside, and two paramedics came rushing in with a stretcher. The Treasury cops asked me where I had the money hidden. I told them there was no money. They asked me where all the money had gone. I told them it was on the other side of the mirror. As I was being wheeled outside to the ambulance, the stretcher went rolling by the bathroom. I watched as an agent began to remove the mirror from the wall. I laughed at myself. Anna walked with the stretcher holding my hand the whole time. They put me in the ambulance and were about to slam the door when the agent who had been talking to me, put his hand on it to stop it from closing. He looked at my wife who was sitting next to the stretcher in the back of the ambulance. Then he looked at me, so you are telling me you know nothing about this. I looked at him as he lifted up five bundles of one-hundred-dollar bills.

I told him it was my money. I asked him where he found it, and he told me it was stuffed under my mattress. I laughed out loud. He told me if it was counterfeit, I was looking at a lot of federal time. I told him he could do whatever he needed to do; it really wasn't going to make a difference. He didn't understand, and I didn't care. The paramedic told him to finish his conversation later and the doors slammed. I felt the ambulance moving and I laid my head back. I felt the prick of a needle in my arm from the other paramedic, and then I passed out. I had never felt as good as I did that day. It was the first day of the rest of my life. Anna told me she loved me, and I replied the same.

She tried to tell me about a malpractice lawsuit before I passed out. The last words from my lips were: "Simplicity is the key to living a healthy life. Stress can be kept to a minimum, if you practice keeping everything, Simple!"

Aftermath

Well, there's my story. I know it is a lot to handle or believe for that matter. But it is true. I lived it. I have the gunshots, broken nose, missing finger and toe to prove it. It turns out the Treasury Department had nothing on me, so they did not pursue any charges against me. They did arrest Dagger on the other side. That was the plan all along, even though I was kept in the dark about it.

The money under the mattress was given back to me because it was not counterfeit. There was twenty-five thousand dollars stuffed under the mattress, and I gladly gave it to myself a few days later. Dagger was sentenced to thirty years in the federal penitentiary because the money that he had in his possession was counterfeit. The serial numbers on the bills had already existed on the other side. The money I gave myself was also counterfeit, but my reflection gave it to Anna and told her to get out of the country, which she did, and in the process, my Anna left me.

Anna left in January. Right after the holidays were over. She wasn't able to handle the stress of my psych ward admittance. I acted crazy for a long time. Hell, maybe I wasn't acting. I made an agreement with myself. I get in trouble a little more now, in order to keep the balance between us. The problem was that I was doing too many good things in life, and my reflection always got the short end of the stick. Neither one of us is better off, but we are happy. I would rather have an exciting life, than a normal routine anyway. I learned that during this episode.

I would love to stay and chat and fill you in more about the whole situation, but I told you the week of hell I had to go through to find my true self. I just want to say, whenever you look at yourself in the mirror, Be Kind! They are going through the same things you are, just in a different way. I wanted to tell people this story because it is important to know what you have inside your mind. If you forget who you are, or do take yourself for granted, all I can say is be careful, because you are the only person watching.

Printed in the United States
by Baker & Taylor Publisher Services

Printed in the United States
by Baker & Taylor Publisher Services

Printed in the United States
by Baker & Taylor Publisher Services

Printed in the United States
by Baker & Taylor Publisher Services